ASTRID'S WAR: ATTACK ON THE USS VALLEY FORGE

ASTRID'S WAR: ATTACK ON THE USS VALLEY FORGE

BOOK ONE OF THE ASTRID AMUNDSEN MILITARY SCIENCE FICTION SERIES

ALAN HOUSEHOLDER

Copyright © 2019 by Alan Householder
All rights reserved.
Printed and manufactured
in the United States of America.

Softcover ISBN: 978-1-7335153-1-3

This is a work of fiction. The characters and events in this work are products of the author's creativity and imagination. Any similarity to actual people (living or not) or events is unintentional and coincidental. Exceptions: Any actual historical events and people mentioned herein are used in a fictitious manner.

To the memory of my sister, Diana

CONTENTS

PROLOGUE

Readers tend to skip prologues, so I will keep this one short.

I was sent to war when I was a fourth-year student at the Naval Academy. I was surprised at how many of the choices I had to make as a midshipman in combat involved ethical dilemmas.

I don't think I ever made a decision as to which fellow-crewmen should live and which should die, though some people might see things differently. As to the enemy, it's a different story entirely.

Whether I always made the right choices, or whether right or wrong choices even existed, remains an open question.

—Astrid Amundsen
November 2370

1

NO REST FOR THE WEARY

We headed back to the USS *Valley Forge* after some mock dogfights. Space can be beautiful, but the preceding hour had been nothing more than flying in nearly absolute blackness, trying to gain missile locks on my team members, and avoiding them getting locks on me.

The only lights visible outside of my cockpit were the stars of the Milky Way and occasional glimpses of the rocket blasts of my friends' interceptors.

It had been a wearying hour of my feet slamming down on pedals and my hands yanking on the control wheel.

Lennox was out in front of me. I was about ten miles behind her. Nash was the same distance behind me. When we were two hundred miles out, we flipped our interceptors, so that we were pointed away from the *Valley Forge*. Then we relit our engines and began deceleration.

A few seconds after my engines ignited, an alarm

sounded from the main control-panel of my Banshee—a rapid series of short tones.

This indicated that I had been picked up by a Kerleegan detection sweep. Navy intelligence held that there were no Kerleegans within light-years of us, so the alarm seemed to be a malfunction or a false positive.

I shut down the alarm, and I said, "Lennox, did you get that alert? What's your radar show?" Of the dozen or so functioning Banshees assigned to the *Valley Forge*, the one piloted by Lennox had the most-advanced sensors.

Lennox took a little time before replying. Finally, she said, "Amundsen, I'm seeing what looks like a group of enemy ships less than three hundred thousand miles out."

That wasn't good news. I said, "We can look closer when we arrive back on the *Valley Forge*. For now, I'm contacting Rabinowitz."

I transmitted a coded message to Commander Rabinowitz, who was second in command and in charge of navigation and weapons.

My mental state had taken an abrupt turn. I had been tired but happy—and looking forward to some sleep. Now I was alert, on edge, and with an urgent need to find out what the *Valley Forge*'s sensors were saying.

I ARRIVED at the *Valley Forge*'s port fighter-bay immediately after Lennox, who had already entered. I used my reaction-control thrusters to move my Banshee into position for entering the bay. My cameras showed me that Nash was right behind me.

I nudged my interceptor forward, through the ship-permeable forcefield that maintained the pressure within the bay. I set my Banshee down and engaged the magnets, then climbed out of the cockpit and hopped to the deck.

I was in a hurry to get to the midshipmen's ready-room, so that I could check the readouts on the *Valley Forge*'s sensors.

~

THE THREE OF US—LENNOX, Nash, and I—soon were together in the ready-room.

Adler and Boyle were still outside in their Banshees. When the rest of us had headed back to the *Valley Forge*, those two still had propellant left, and they wanted to make sure they burned it up.

The ready-room had an elaborate navigation console, with several monitors showing the output of the *Valley Forge*'s detection array. I punched a few keys and brought up the medium-range display.

Lennox and Nash sat in their usual chairs, which were near the holo-table.

I said, "I don't think there was a malfunction. I'm seeing a cluster of ships, not much over two hundred thousand miles out. Our navigation and weapons people must already be on top of this."

Plainly, we were facing a Kerleegan task force.

I was about to follow up with Rabinowitz, but then we heard a knock on the bulkhead next to the ready-room hatch, and standing in the hatchway was Captain Jefferson.

We don't normally salute under such circumstances, but I did call out, "Officer on the deck, attention to orders!"

Jefferson said, "As you were," as he entered the ready-room. He was wearing an EVA (extravehicular activity) suit, and he held his helmet under his arm.

I said, "Good evening, Captain Jefferson." We don't have evenings in space, of course, but on the *Valley Forge* everything was synced to UTC +0. "I gather you were outside of the ship?"

Jefferson said, "Yes, one of the dorsal guns wasn't rotating, and the mechanics were stumped. I took care of it."

I said, "Sounds good." But actually, I thought that sounded highly weird. When does the captain of a warship go out alone to make repairs on a gun mount?

Never.

Lennox said, "What may we do for you?"

Jefferson said, "We've picked up images of a Kerleegan task force in the area. Half a dozen carriers and several cruisers. Not sure what they're up to. But stay on your toes."

Nash said, "We received similar indications when we were out in our Banshees. We thought it might be a malfunction of the sensors."

Jefferson said, "No malfunction."

I said, "Right, we confirmed that. I was about to contact Commander Rabinowitz."

Jefferson said, "I'm headed to the bridge right now, to discuss navigation with her. Be ready for anything."

We all exchanged a few more words with the captain, and soon he departed.

Nash said, "What's he mean, 'be ready for anything'? That sounds almost like he expects a battle."

Lennox said, "This *is* a warship. We *are* at war."

Nash said, "I'm talking about prudence. We're one lonesome little cruiser. They are six carriers and multiple other ships. We have a handful of interceptors. They have hundreds. I hope Jefferson isn't considering engaging these guys. For us midshipmen, this was supposed to be a training mission, not a combat mission."

I said, "We're in the Navy, Nash. We don't get to decide what we're going to do."

Nash said, "No argument there."

2

SUMMONED TO THE BRIDGE

I knew Nash quite well, and I realized that what he said was valid. He wasn't concerned about himself. Nash was aggressive in everything having to do with training or battle. He had entered the Naval Academy after a stint as a crewman on a destroyer, and he had already been involved in clashes with the Kerleegans, as a turret gunner. He had been awarded the Silver Star for valor.

Addressing me by my first name, Nash said, "Astrid, can you tell which direction they're headed? Maybe they're moving away at high speed."

Lennox clapped her hands twice and said, "Nash! Quit thinking so much!"

I studied the monitors and then said, "They're headed in our direction. They're not accelerating, but they're doing a good sixty miles per second. They're not on a collision course, but they'll come close if they don't change their course or speed."

Nash said seriously, "How close to us will their present course bring them?"

"Looks like about ten thousand miles," I said. "And they'll be here in about an hour. Less, if they light their engines."

Then came a brief high-pitched tone over the ready-room speakers, followed by Captain Jefferson's voice. "Midshipman Astrid Amundsen, to the bridge in ten minutes."

I clicked onto Jefferson's comm line and said, "Aye aye, Sir." I looked at the others and shrugged.

Nash was the smallest of our group. I always wondered how a guy so little and light made it into the Naval Academy. He said, "This looks like an opportunity for you, Astrid. Keep moving up the ladder of success, and you might be worthy of me taking you out to dinner when we get back to the Academy."

Nash was a nice guy, always respectful, and I knew he was kidding around. I almost started to put together a witty response, but then Lennox spoke up.

"Nash, problem is, you'd have to do away with Joseph first. And I don't think you're up to that. Little guy like you? Joseph would drop-kick you out of the yard."

Lennox was referring to Joseph Stone, my fiancé. He had graduated from Annapolis a few years earlier, and we were to be married soon after my own graduation.

I said, "I don't know, Lennox. I might be up for a free meal—if I prove worthy." I turned toward Nash and said, "Thanks, Nash, that'll give me something to shoot for."

Nash nodded, then looked at Lennox and said, "There you go, Lennox."

Lennox shook her head in mock disgust and said, "If Astrid *ever* allows you to take her to dinner, *I'll* pick up the tab."

"Fine," Nash said. "Start saving your money."

Both Nash and Lennox made a couple more wisecracks as I straightened my uniform in preparation for reporting to the bridge. The three of us, as well as Adler and Boyle, were on the *Valley Forge* for a three-week cruise during our fourth year at the Naval Academy. We knew each other well, and we liked to joke around.

I reached for the hatch, and Nash said, "Word to the wise, though, Amundsen." He took a bite out of a candy bar, then said, "Jefferson's on the rampage again."

"Rampage?" I asked. "He seemed okay when he stopped by here."

Nash said, "Right, but his normal state is on the meaner side. I saw him chewing out your pal Waters a few hours ago."

"What for?"

"Probably nothing," Nash said. "Pretty sure the captain mistook Waters for somebody else. He called him by some other name. I didn't catch the details. I was concentrating on blending into the background. Anyhow, Waters sowed the wind, and now *you're* going to reap the hurricane."

Lennox said, "You mean reap the *whirlwind*."

Nash shrugged. "With Jefferson, it's gonna be a hurricane."

I didn't say anything. Lieutenant Waters was one of the eight Marine pilots assigned to the *Valley Forge*. He had taken me under his wing—I knew him from when he was at the Academy. He had showed me and the others some of the ropes on the *Valley Forge*. We midshipmen had received training, but we lacked practical experience. Well, Lennox, Adler, and I lacked experience. As I already mentioned, Nash had served before he came to

Annapolis. The same applied to Boyle, who had served with Nash.

Lennox tapped a few input keys on her wrist-computer. She said, "I'm going to bring up some visuals." The tabletop began to glow.

Above the square surface, as though resting on it, a cubical 3D-image appeared. It looked like an ordinary hologram, though the technology behind it was different.

Lennox reached into the image and pointed at a cluster of red specks near an upper corner.

"Well, well," she said. "These are the Kerleegan warships." Near a lower corner of the cube was a single blue speck. She pointed to it and said, "This is us." Lennox looked at her wrist. "Here, I'll sync up the stats with your wrist-computers. You can both track speed and distance all you want." She hit more keys.

In outer-space terms, a couple hundred thousand miles is kissing distance. And it looked like the Kerleegans might be leaning in to give us a peck on the cheek. My feeling of exhaustion was now a fading memory. A survival instinct had taken over.

Nash and Lennox also seemed hyper-alert.

We hadn't expected to see enemy activity on this trip.

Again, Lennox consulted her wrist-computer. "They've slowed a little. They're down to forty-two miles per second, relative to us. I suspect that means that they see us."

Nash asked, "What took us so long to see *them*?"

"I'm sure they were running super-cold," Lennox said. "All engines were off. Now their engines are on, for deceleration."

Lennox was an expert at manipulating 3D projections. She reached toward the enemy ships with both hands, then drew her hands apart, and the sector with the enemy craft now filled the cube.

I didn't like what I saw. It was as though we were looking into a cubical aquarium, four feet in each dimension.

Eleven fish were swimming in the tank—fish shaped like Kerleegan starships.

They were scattered throughout the cube. Six of them were large. Five were smaller. The bigger ones were three times the length of the smaller.

I felt as though I had entered a nightmare.

3

LONG ODDS

Rather calmly considering the circumstances, Lennox said, "Looks like six carriers and five cruisers. That's consistent with what Captain Jefferson told us."

Okay, I thought, *eleven enemy ships versus our one ship. Those aren't bad odds*.

I don't know whether it was lack of sleep, or what, but next it occurred to me that I had overlooked a couple of things.

First: Correct, eleven-to-one odds aren't bad. They're *horrible*.

Second, in terms of "strength of force," a carrier is considered the equivalent of at least four cruisers.

That made the effective odds against us twenty-nine to one. I said, "And now they're less than an hour away."

Lennox shrugged. "Depends on how much they brake. Then again, once they figure out what they want to do, they may well accelerate."

I said, "And much less time than that till we're within

effective range of their missiles." I glanced at my watch. "I gotta get going."

Nash held up an index finger to get my attention and said, "Jefferson was one of your instructors in strategy two years back, wasn't he?"

I said, "Right, we called him the Smiling Assassin. It didn't really fit."

Nash said, "It didn't?"

"Right," I said. "Nobody ever saw him smile."

I MOVED OUT BRISKLY. I hadn't eaten any dinner, but I wasn't hungry. I was focused only on the things Lennox, Nash, and I had been talking about, and on the fact that I needed to get to the bridge quickly.

Jefferson probably wanted to show me what it's like to plan strategy in the real world. As Nash implied, the reason Jefferson singled me out was certainly that I had been one of his students in strategy, and in fact, one of his best.

I wished that Adler and Boyle had been with us in the ready-room. Nash and Lennox would fill them in, though, when they got back. I thought about something Adler had said to me a few days earlier.

"The *Valley Forge* is a toy boat in a bathtub, Astrid," Adler had said. "If we run into any Kerleegans, I'm sure Jefferson has instructions to return us safely to the Naval Academy."

I didn't argue with Adler at the time, but I was sure he was wrong. For us, this voyage was part of a new program at the Academy, supposedly designed to give the midshipmen experience on actual Navy vessels before graduation. It was widely believed that this program was simply a way of supplying our ships with the manpower they needed. That was certainly my own belief.

The Kerleegans hailed from a planet in a faraway solar system. Strange to say, we didn't know the location of their home planet. It was further away from our planet than thirty light-years, though. Our own detailed explorations included all planetary systems within that distance from Earth. Beyond that, it was essentially a "here be dragons" zone.

Given this lack of information about the Kerleegan place of origin, all we knew of them and their ways and motives came from observing their military actions. They seemed to be one of those spacefaring nations that loves to roam about the galaxy demonstrating what they perceive to be their ascendancy over all other sentient life. We imagine that they are taking over colonies at the outskirts of explored space. And people make this claim about them. But I have never seen incontrovertible proof of this.

What we do know is that they don't hesitate to engage starships that are based on Earth, though they have not actually come near to Earth. Most nations on Earth seem to adopt the attitude that the Kerleegans should not be considered a threat unless and until they actually arrive within the solar system.

To me it seems those nations are playing a fool's game. I guess I can say that our national policy agrees with me, since we have a super-fleet protecting Earth, as well as large fleets assigned to our colonies on the Moon and Mars. As for Earth's outposts on other planets in this section of the galaxy, they are essentially without meaningful defense, but none have been threatened yet.

Anyway, our assignment *did* involve combat, potentially. We were all at least twenty years old, and Nash and Boyle were twenty-two or twenty-three, so it isn't as though the Navy was sending children to war. Nobody ever guaranteed to keep us safe.

I CONTINUED TOWARD THE BRIDGE. I knew the route. It involved several long walkways and corridors. In this area, the innards of the *Valley Forge* looked like a cross between a manufacturing plant and a metalworking shop. Other parts of the ship, such as our reactors, engines, and weapons systems, were enclosed and well protected. In all, the ship carried hundreds of missiles, and of course it had a great deal of other weaponry, including guns and drones. And that takes up a lot of space.

Then there was a final short corridor that led to the bridge's entry. The hatch was open. Standing guard outside the bridge was one of the Marines assigned to the *Valley Forge*. Their primary duty was as pilots of the Banshee fighter-craft, and as Marines they were largely independent of the crew. But they also served in other capacities, sometimes in ship security and as backup turret-gunners.

4

HATED AND FEARED

The Marine at the bridge was Lieutenant Waters—the man Nash mentioned earlier. Waters and I were on a first-name basis. Well, he usually called me *Astrid,* but I never called him anything other than *Waters.* He was an Academy graduate.

I had met him there during Plebe Summer, in June 2366. "Met" is probably the wrong word. He was the detailer assigned to my group during the first half of the summer. He yelled at us a lot and ran us ragged. But later, he and I became friends. I saluted him, and he rolled his eyes back toward the bridge, subtly. He said, "Good morning, Midshipman Amundsen."

I knew from his eye-rolling that Waters was following strict protocols only because Captain Jefferson was on the bridge. Jefferson was a known stickler for procedures and technicalities, and when he was around, everyone was on edge. This applied to us midshipmen as well. After all, we were naval officers under his command. Additionally, as midshipmen we were just about the lowliest officers in the Navy. We were in no position to complain.

Upon entering the bridge, I reported to Captain Jefferson and saluted him and the other officers present—Commander Rabinowitz, who was the executive officer, and two other officers. These other two were Lieutenant Commanders Silver and Newton. I was acquainted with all of them.

Captain Jefferson said, "Midshipman Amundsen, take a look at this." He gestured toward the center monitor in a bank of five large monitors.

Jefferson was a burly guy, late-fifties. He had dark skin and black hair, which was graying in places. I know he was born in Massachusetts, but I've heard that his ancestors came from the Armenian Highlands of Western Asia. He had a beautiful, clear voice, and he spoke perfect English, with a slight New England accent.

I had never heard anyone say anything nice about Jefferson. Interestingly, all of the criticisms boiled down to him not being much of a people person. Those who served under him were always on tenterhooks, and they tended to find solidarity in the fact that he was grinding *all* of them down. No one received special treatment.

My own views concerning the man were highly conflicted. I knew him better than most did, because of the fact that I had attended classes led by him. He was strict, but I had several discussions with him outside of class hours, and he told me more than once that I was the best student he had ever taught. It's hard to dislike someone who tells you that. And I saw the frustrations he experienced in dealing with students who weren't all that interested.

He was one of the most hated and feared instructors at the Academy. The administration loved him, because he was a war hero. Having him on the faculty was a public-relations triumph for the Academy. But his real love was combat, and he went back to captaining warships at the end of my second year at the Academy.

He had a line that he loved to use on the rare occasions that someone was unprepared in class. He would say, "Midshipman Jones, I think it's time for us to start cutting some of the dead wood out of the tree that is this classroom."

That image flitted through my mind when, as directed, I looked at the monitor. In the lower left-hand corner of the screen was a small blue icon representing the *Valley Forge*. Around it at regular distances were a series of concentric circles. In the upper-right corner were eleven red icons with similar circles. Red was ordinarily used to designate enemy ships or unidentified ships. The circles in each group were separated by distances that represented twenty thousand miles.

5

ELEVEN RED ICONS

Like the ready-room, the bridge was home to a holo-table. Jefferson said, "Let me bring it up on the table." He pressed a few keys, and then the same 3D picture that Lennox had created arose, except that this one showed much higher definition.

I had no clue what my response was supposed to be. I said, "I see." That seemed about as harmless a remark as I could make.

Jefferson said, "Well, you're looking, but do you really *see?*"

And now you are probably beginning to understand why Captain Jefferson was widely loathed. Personally, because of my history with him, I was able to accept Jefferson and his ways, but one of my pet peeves in life is people who dance around with what they're saying, when they easily could come out and tell you what they want you to know.

I said, "I don't think I do." This, I believed, was safer than guessing.

Jefferson said, "These red icons represent eleven

Kerleegan warships. Specifically, they represent six carriers and five cruisers."

I said, "Makes sense. Midshipman Lennox showed me similar images, and she broke them down the same way. But this image is much clearer."

I began to feel acute distress. Being outnumbered eleven ships to one will do that to a person. I tend toward catastrophic thinking, and I pictured my head on a Kerleegan pike, along with the heads of my fellow midshipmen and those of the other officers on the bridge.

I wondered why Jefferson was discussing these things so calmly with me, when the enemy task force was drawing near at high speed.

I was sure Jefferson and the other officers present were aware of the urgency of the situation. Did Jefferson want me to mention that? I decided to do so, and I said, "We're almost within range of the enemy scanners, if we aren't there already." Based on what Lennox had said, I was actually quite sure that they already had detected us.

"Yes," Jefferson said, looking directly into my eyes. "That's what I'm getting at. We're in a situation that calls for close analysis. You'll find this instructive."

Jefferson turned to look intently at the monitor. He stared at it for a solid minute. No one said anything.

Jefferson was breathing deeply. His face was covered with perspiration. This was not normal for him.

Commander Rabinowitz, whom I knew to be smart and wise, looked at me. Almost imperceptibly, she moved her head back and forth. I had no doubt that this was intended to tell me that something was seriously wrong with what the captain was doing.

I figured that I had arrived after some kind of confrontation between the captain and the rest of the bridge crew. Jefferson probably had been engaging in odd behavior for a while before he summoned me. In fact, I now questioned the rationality of his solo spacewalk to fix the gun turret. Jefferson was the last person on the ship who should have been out there on such a task. I had entered the bridge to become part of a story's climax, without knowing the rest of the story.

Then I looked at Silver and Newton. Their somber expressions and their silence communicated volumes.

All of that confirmed my speculations.

I pondered the scenario. Jefferson was the man, the kahuna, the top of the heap when it came to strategy. Here we were in the earliest stages of a possible confrontation with the Kerleegans, and all three of the other bridge-officers—each a commander or lieutenant commander of long experience—were questioning Jefferson's approach.

The weird thing was that Jefferson *did* seem to be acting strangely, even for him. Also peculiar was the fact that the others all seemed to think it was important that they communicate their belief to me. It was as though they were saying, *Astrid! You're the only one who can do anything about this! Help us!*

All right, so there were eleven Kerleegan vessels, and one American vessel. With experience, a captain can make a good judgment, even in borderline cases, as to whether or not he should engage the enemy. Our technology was more advanced than that of the Kerleegans, but they had far more ships and personnel. This being the case, our overall strategy in the war was to choose our battles carefully, and only engage when the odds favored us heavily and we were confident that we would suffer few if any losses.

It was pretty much an axiom that we would win this war. The question was, how many lives and ships would we lose before that time came?

The Kerleegan philosophy was the opposite. They wanted to engage us at every opportunity. There have been cases in which our force has been far superior to that of the Kerleegans, yet they have gone out of their way to engage us. Even if we destroy three or four of their ships for each one of ours that they destroy, we will run out of ships and sailors long before they do. Neither of us will run out of ships any time soon, though.

Usually, our ships travel in packs. The reason the *Valley Forge* was a lone wolf is that, on paper, this was a training voyage. For most of us midshipmen, it was the first taste we had of real operations. We had been told that we were going to a region of space where no enemy activity was expected.

Honestly, I thought the brass back in DC *knew* that there were Kerleegan ships in this area, or at least expected some. I believed that we on the *Valley Forge* were simply bait, or a target sent by the Navy to bring the Kerleegans out of hiding. If true, this would mean that there was a large US strike force within attack distance—though it could be a day or more away from us.

With their powerful sensors, such a strike force could keep an eye on us. If a small-sized task force of Kerleegans descended on the *Valley Forge*, a large US force could descend and defeat the enemy, though that might be curtains for the *Valley Forge*. This was guesswork on my part, but it made perfect sense. The *Valley Forge* was no more than a sacrificial lamb.

After all, the *Valley Forge* was only a hundred eighty-two yards from bow to stern. That's a good size when there's no comparison being made, and the ship definitely presents an imposing appearance when viewed by itself. But Joseph, my husband-to-be, was stationed on the USS *Constellation*. The *Constellation* was more than twice that length, and its fighting capacity was greater by an order of magnitude.

The *Valley Forge*'s crew of about two hundred was more like a skeleton crew. The *Constellation*'s crew was ten times ours in number. Joseph's ship was part of a task force. Mine was entirely alone.

6

COMBAT MODELS AND CAPTAIN JEFFERSON

The *Valley Forge* had a combat model, which was its analytical method for determining a force's likelihood of success under a predetermined set of circumstances. You plug-in a large number of variables, and do some calculations, and the results you receive back show your odds of prevailing, along with the likely reduction of the combatant forces, and other projections. Initially, what you want is a "fight or flee" recommendation.

To "flee" sounds bad, but it's not. We normally call it breaking off contact. In the present war, as I mentioned, we always are looking for a huge advantage before engaging the enemy. Roughly speaking, we're looking for the equivalent of a seven-to-one advantage in strength of force, and something like a ninety-nine percent—or better—chance of victory in the engagement.

In combat involving starships, the normal model is the salvo combat-model devised long ago by Hughes. Different captains put their own spin on it. Jefferson had his version of it, which everyone called the "Jefferson model." Jefferson had a dozen tweaks that he applied to the Hughes model, and he taught those in depth in the strategy class he led at the Academy.

Of course, we students were pretty jaded, and we thought we knew everything. Most of us didn't see the logic of Jefferson's modifications to Hughes, and some of us—including me—had put together our own models that we thought would be better than Jefferson's. Of course, our brilliant models, in most cases, were pretty bad.

So THERE I was on the bridge, with Captain Jefferson acting mildly manic, and with his three bridge-officers indicating that problems lay ahead.

Jefferson handed me a one-page printout of the computer's recommendations based on his combat model.

I glanced over the sheet, and as expected it included detailed findings and recommendations—fight or flee, weapons to use, and everything else—down to the exact second that shields should be raised in the event it was decided to join battle.

Jefferson said to me, "Textbook case, Astrid, like those we studied. It's a highly complex scenario. Just the way we like them."

But it didn't seem complex to me. They had six carriers and five cruisers. We had one cruiser, the *Valley Forge*. I didn't need a combat model to tell me we needed to stay away from this enemy task force.

"You see," Jefferson said, "the enemy has concluded a gravity-assist maneuver and their ships are now at zero acceleration. That's key."

The "gravity assist" and "zero acceleration" were "key"?

I'm sure I started looking sick, as though I were going to throw up, since that's how I felt. I was lightheaded, which is particularly bad when you are facing a battle. But all that went away quickly, and I was able to experience my intense fear in all its unadulterated force.

I looked quickly at the other officers, and they were staring at me with their eyes wide-open, as though to say, *See what we mean?*

Something struck me. They were on the verge of mutiny, and they either wanted me to join them, or to be a witness to these circumstances.

And then I had a whole train of other horrible thoughts. I saw the mutineers seize all crewmen who were loyal to the captain, and either execute them, or maroon them, or set them adrift in a lifeboat. Again, I pictured my head on a pike.

Or maybe I'd become one of the mutineers. Mutineers are invariably tracked down—and executed.

I didn't much like either scenario.

I decided to take a risk, and to express my misgivings indirectly. "I suppose that a slight modification of our vector will keep us clear of the enemy ships."

Jefferson said, "Amundsen, no! Didn't you learn *anything* in my class?" His voice exuded disappointment, and maybe disgust.

This time, I decided to play it safe. I said nothing.

Jefferson shook his head and said, "Hopeless." He sat down in front of the monitor and stared at it for about thirty seconds.

Under those circumstances, it seemed like an eternity. I tried to maintain my composure, but I was becoming more and more agitated.

I looked at Jefferson's head. A pronounced cowlick

marred the otherwise perfect contours of his hair. I wondered: Could that cowlick be the cause of his current nuttiness? I had the urge to reach out and try to flatten it. I figured that, just maybe, if I could plaster it down, he would return to normal.

I don't know where that absurd thought came from.

Rabinowitz caught my eye. She patted her sidearm.

And all the while I imagined the Kerleegan ships veering off their present course to intercept us. And I pictured them launching missiles, hundreds of them, with us—with *me*—as the target.

7

COURSE TWENTY-ONE, TWENTY-FIVE

Finally, Jefferson said, "Talos, set course twenty-one, twenty-five."

Talos was the ship's main computer. When Jefferson said "twenty-one, twenty-five," I felt a sense of relief sweep over me. The captain's break with reality was over. Disaster was averted. Lives were preserved.

But then it dawned on me that this was not the format of a normal course change. It was code, and I was afraid that Jefferson was instructing Talos to modify the *Valley Forge*'s course so that it would intercept the enemy ships.

Talos said, "To prevent misunderstanding or error, please repeat the order, and state authorization code."

Jefferson said, "Set course twenty-one, twenty-five. Code two, six, eight, Jefferson, two, two, one."

Talos said nothing.

Jefferson said, "Well?"

Talos said, "Awaiting the executive officer's confirmation of the order."

Jefferson turned toward Rabinowitz and said, "Commander Rabinowitz, go ahead and confirm."

Rabinowitz said, "Sir, for reasons I've already expressed—"

Jefferson interrupted and said, "Are you refusing my lawful order?"

Rabinowitz said, "No, Sir, I'm following protocols. The requirement of confirmation contemplates that I will decide, independent of the captain's order, whether the order to Talos should be confirmed."

At that, Captain Jefferson drew his sidearm from its holster, took off the safety, and racked back the slide.

As I was watching all that, I couldn't believe that it actually was unfolding before me. Even without reloading, Jefferson could put three rounds each into Rabinowitz, Silver, Newton, and me.

In my mind's eye, I saw the scene several hours from now. The confrontation with the enemy had passed. We lost four crewmen—mutinous dogs whom the captain had needed to kill. And the name of one of those dogs was Astrid.

Or maybe we would have a running gun-battle. Jefferson would hunt us down. As we passed through the ship, we would gain allies, who would join us in the struggle. But in this particular nightmare, Jefferson seemed super-human. His sidearm never ran out of ammunition. Bullets bounced off his forehead. The entire crew was doomed.

At least, that's the way I pictured events.

Back in reality, when Jefferson drew his weapon, it was clear to me that he had snapped. I wondered if he was going to shoot officers until he found one who would carry out his order.

Jefferson said, "Talos, what happens if the executive officer is not available?"

"Then the duty to affirm or disaffirm the order falls upon the acting executive officer."

"And if there is no acting executive officer?"

Talos said, "Then the duty falls upon the bridge officer of next-highest rank, and so on, until someone is available."

Jefferson said, "And what if I'm the only officer on the bridge?"

Talos said, "Then the command cannot be carried out."

Jefferson sighed in frustration.

At this point, I felt that I was in the middle of some epic historical event, a mutiny or near mutiny against a commanding officer who plainly had taken leave of his senses. I was also certain that I wouldn't live to tell this story unless the mutiny were carried out.

Jefferson said, "Tell me this, Talos. Are there any circumstances under which you will carry out my order without confirmation by another officer?"

"No, Sir, there are none."

"All right, Talos," Jefferson said. He holstered his weapon and then said, "Please give over all navigation functions to Commander Rabinowitz."

Talos said, "Yes, Sir. Done."

Jefferson then looked at Rabinowitz and said, "Commander Rabinowitz, implement the order I gave to Talos, and do so immediately."

Rabinowitz said, "I'm sorry, Captain Jefferson, but I don't think I can do that."

Jefferson called out to Waters, who was still on duty just off the bridge. "Lieutenant Waters, please take Commander Rabinowitz into custody, and place her in a cell in the brig."

That was an odd request. If Jefferson was going to have someone take Commander Rabinowitz into custody, it should be a Navy master-at-arms, since they are more like military police. Not only that, but the Marines weren't even in Jefferson's chain of command.

I was pretty sure, though, that Waters would obey, in part because of professional courtesy, but in part because Waters would rather that he himself carry out the order. That way he could bend the rules if he thought it was necessary.

And sure enough, Waters entered the bridge, and he departed with Commander Rabinowitz walking civilly beside him.

Again, I glanced at my wrist-computer. With each minute that passed, the Kerleegan formation was over two thousand miles closer. The *Valley Forge*'s present course wasn't the most direct route toward the enemy. But it was contributing to the enemy's rapid approach.

What we really needed was for the *Valley Forge* to move decisively away from the Kerleegan ships, on a carefully crafted course. Killing our stern engines and lighting our reverse-thrust bow-engines wouldn't be the perfect approach, but it would be a lot better than what we were doing.

My main concern was that, even if we didn't implement the captain's insane plan of directly approaching the enemy, the passage of time would bring about the same result.

We definitely were within range of the enemy's sensors. We were also within range of their missiles, but they would want to come in closer before launching. Inevitably, though, several things would happen soon.

First, the enemy would change course to intercept us,

if they had not done so already. Second, when they reached optimum range, they would launch missiles and fighters. And third, if they could disable most of our weapons systems, or cause us to exhaust our missiles, they would board us. We were thoroughly outmatched, so this last possibility was what amounted to a certainty.

As for Captain Jefferson, he had taken Rabinowitz's seat. He was pressing keys on the navigation console, and I figured he had done his best to implement the course change that he wanted. I wondered whether Talos was programmed to alter such an ill-advised course.

Soon it wouldn't matter. We would be in a battle, eleven ships against one.

8

BAD NEWS FOR MY FRIENDS

I wasn't sure how things were going to play out, but I wanted to get back to my friends, so that I could warn them of what was happening and give them time to prepare.

I knew that if we survived the initial onslaught by the Kerleegans, they would board us.

We had been trained at Annapolis on techniques for repelling boarders, but now it was imperative that the five of us prepare ourselves mentally for becoming life takers, not merely in theory, but in practice. I knew that Adler's view—that the Navy wouldn't put students at risk—was shared by most of the others. Not by me. That's not the way the Navy operates.

I said, "Captain Jefferson, may I have permission to return to the other midshipmen? Since we're going into battle, I'd like to be permitted to make final preparations with them."

Jefferson stared coldly into my eyes.

The bridge was absolutely silent. I was pretty sure his mind was working overtime, trying to interpret what I had said as being insubordinate or insolent. And to be honest, I was wondering myself whether there was something like that in what I said, or in how I said it.

But at last, Jefferson said, "Of course, Midshipman Amundsen. Return to your people. Prepare them for the conflict. We're going to win this. *Semper fortis.*"

Regardless of what the captain had said, you can be sure that in my mental state I would consider his words as the ravings of a madman. It was a little subtle, but I think what he said definitely qualified.

At any rate, I said, "Aye aye, Sir. *Semper fortis.*"

I was out of there before he had a chance to change his mind.

I hated to leave Jefferson's bridge-officers on their own. But realistically there was nothing I could do. It was like watching two trains approaching each other, on the same track, in slow motion. I was hoping that those other officers would jump onto both trains and throw the brake levers. But I knew that was unlikely.

Then something else dawned on me. Would the other bridge-officers try to restrain the captain physically? I hoped that they would. But I had a rock-solid belief that they wouldn't.

The captain was forcing us into a suicide run that would gain us nothing and would result in the loss of two hundred sailors and a warship. That was the real-life thing that was happening.

But looked at clinically, academically, and legally, our situation was merely a case of a captain leading his ship and crew into a battle against a superior force. That's all. Nothing against that in the regulations. Absolutely no grounds for mutiny or even insubordination. *That* was the real problem.

The other officers might be a little resistant, and grumble, and be slow about carrying out orders, but they were not going to go beyond that. And as much as I disapproved of Jefferson's approach, *he* was the captain—not me, and not the other bridge-officers.

I was willing to die for my country, and I half-expected that I would someday. But I didn't want to die before I even graduated from Annapolis.

Then I thought about my fiancé, Joseph. I wondered what his reaction would be to the conduct of Captain Jefferson. I liked to think that if Joseph had known, he would commandeer the *Constellation*, and make a mad dash to save us—because of me. But he was light-years away, and he likely pictured me sound asleep, or perhaps listening to a lecture on safety procedures.

Next, I thought more clearly about my chances of surviving this debacle. Factoring-in all of the paths that led to survival, I grew more optimistic. Jefferson might change his mind. *Somebody*—even if not the bridge officers—might wrest control of the ship from Jefferson. The Kerleegans might have bigger fish to fry somewhere. Or some other event might save me. I put my chances of survival at about three in ten.

Maybe a little less.

As I continued to move toward the ready-room, I wondered what was happening on the bridge. The captain had instructed Lieutenant Waters to arrest Commander Rabinowitz, the executive officer. I wondered if the same fate would befall the other two bridge officers, Silver and Newton.

I didn't have to wait long for my answer to that question. As I was moving aft, I crossed paths with three Marines. We midshipmen came into frequent contact with the Marines, since they were a friendly bunch—*if they liked you.*

Actually, as Marines, they weren't even part of the crew *per se*. They welcomed outsiders like us—especially me, since I intended to go into the Marines myself, as did my father and his father. And as I mentioned, I knew Waters from Annapolis. I'm pretty sure he told the other Marines that we were okay. I knew all of them by first name.

The three coming toward me were softly grumbling to each other until they saw me. One of them laughed and said, "There she is, guys. Cuff her and get her to the brig."

Another said, "No, Alec, just the ones on the bridge."

I came to a stop, and so did they. "What's going on?"

Alec said, "We should ask *you* that, Astrid. Waters has the XO in custody. We're on our way to arrest Silver and Newton."

I shook my head and said, "Great, just great."

One of the others, Rupert by name, asked, "Astrid, what on Earth is happening?"

I summarized the facts, and stressed that we were likely in for the fight of our lives against the Kerleegans.

Alec said, "Shotguns, Astrid, shotguns. For the boarders."

I said, "I hear you." I paused a second, then said, "Okay guys, fair winds." Even though there was no wind in space, this was a farewell we often used.

They wished me the same, and then they were on their way.

The reference to shotguns was ominous. I hadn't mentioned boarders, but the Marines immediately put two and two together.

All of the officers, including us lowly midshipmen,

possessed sidearms. We were also issued M90s, which were compact assault-rifles with fifty-round magazines.

But the *preferred* weapon for use against boarding parties was the shotgun. And the *Valley Forge* had plenty of them. All of our ships had shotgun racks placed at intervals throughout. Each rack normally held eight shotguns with special magazines holding twenty-four rounds. The rounds alternated buckshot and slugs, so each magazine carried twelve of each.

9

GENERAL QUARTERS! ALL HANDS, MAN YOUR BATTLE STATIONS

When I arrived back at the ready-room, Adler and Boyle had returned from their exercise. Those two, and Nash also, were laughing, throwing paper wads at each other, and generally wasting time.

I surveyed the scene, feeling a little discouraged. These were the people the Naval Academy was sending against the Kerleegans.

Finally, people noticed that I was just standing there.

Boyle asked, "What's up, Amundsen?"

All of them quieted down. I guess I looked serious.

"Astrid," Nash asked, "what's going on?"

"We're about to see action against the Kerleegans," I said. "It's six carriers and five cruisers against us. Haven't you been tracking all this?"

Lennox said, "*I* have. My provisional assumption was that we would be breaking off contact. When I first saw the enemy ships, I thought we would see combat, but after you left, I thought it through further, and I concluded there was no way of that happening. But now they're accelerating."

Adler said, "Eleven ships against the *Valley Forge*? Lennox is right. Shouldn't we be breaking off?"

I said, "We *should*, but Captain Jefferson doesn't see it that way. Rabinowitz, Silver, and Newton are in the brig, or headed there."

Boyle forced a laugh and said, "She's joking, guys."

Adler thought he had an "ah ha" moment—he now was sure I was fooling—and he said, "It's not funny, Astrid."

I locked eyes with him and said, "Do I look like I'm kidding? We have to get a line on EVA suits and be ready for general quarters."

The others all looked at one another.

I headed toward one of the lockers, opened it, and began to pull out an EVA suit, including a helmet. The EVA suits would protect us from decompression, which was likely to affect large sections of the ship if the hull were breached.

Lennox joined me and did the same thing. She said to the others, "Astrid's not joking."

Adler said, "Are you in on this, too, Lennox?"

Lennox stared at him grimly and said, "Adler, stop being an idiot and get with the program."

Boyle said, semi-seriously, "Attention, all crew. This is your captain. We're all going to die." He joined us at the locker, and soon Adler and Nash did the same.

The EVA suits were close-fitting, but they were made to go on over normal uniforms, after we removed our shoulder holsters. Still, I took off my long-sleeved camouflage shirt, but kept my T-shirt. So did the others. For the time being, we left our helmets off.

As though he had the right to complain about the enemy's strategy, Nash said, "Why would the Kerleegans want to bother with a ship like the *Valley Forge*, anyway? Seems like a waste of manpower and weapons. We'll do far more damage to them than they will to us."

I said, "Percentage-wise, that's a doubtful assertion."

Nash persisted. "But why attack us at all?"

I said, "I assume they want our faster-than-light drive."

"We don't *have* an FTL drive," Nash said.

I said, "I know that, and you know that, but the Kerleegans don't."

We had piggy-backed on an FTL-equipped ship, which had dropped us off and departed.

The Kerleegans were known to have at least two types of FTL drives. Ours were more effective in just about every way, and seizing one was a high priority for them.

Nash said, "Rotten luck."

I tried to come up with something by way of refuting that, but I failed. All I could say was, "Got *that* right."

By this time, the enemy likely would have broken from their course, and they probably were accelerating. They might be moving sixty or more miles per second, closing on us at over three thousand miles *each minute*. At this point they would probably try to maximize their speed, to impart just that much more velocity to their missiles.

After launching the first group of missiles, they were apt to decelerate. They could do this rapidly by killing the engines, rotating their ships a hundred and eighty degrees, and relighting the engines. Or for ships having forward-facing bow engines, as did the *Valley Forge*, you can kill your stern engines and light the bow engines. Those were my thoughts as I donned my EVA suit.

Adler was breathing deeply, and I was afraid that he was going to have a panic attack. But he pushed onward and got his EVA suit on. Nash seemed a little confused and shaky. He picked up three different helmets before settling on one he liked—though all were identical. But it seemed that both guys were okay.

I started to wonder—maybe the Kerleegans would move on. Maybe they weren't interested in engaging us. Maybe we were mobilizing for no reason.

Then the klaxon sounded.

It was a harsh alarm-tone that repeated rapidly, twice per second. After a dozen seconds, the alarm stopped, and a recorded male voice came over the ship's main channel, with this bone-chilling announcement: "General quarters, general quarters. All hands, man your battle stations. Set Condition Zebra throughout the ship. Incoming missiles and incoming fighters."

Then that whole routine, the alarm and the announcement, repeated.

10

ONE FOR THE BOOKS

We knew that soon most or all of us would almost certainly be dead. At this point our opportunity to break off contact was gone. The battle was on, and enemy missiles and fighters would be on us soon. I hadn't really prepared myself for this. I knew that combat had been a possibility, but I assumed that I would not be led into it by a madman.

I hadn't said *real* goodbyes to my relatives or to Joseph. I had said farewells for the time being, and my family probably had been worrying about me, but they never would have imagined events like these.

As for friends, other than my fellow midshipmen, and my fiancé, of course, I didn't really have any. But I've always been something of a loner. I love spending time by myself. For entertainment, I like to read. Never really went out much. My family lived near San Diego. My parents are still there. I saw a lot of ships, and that was great, and that might have laid the groundwork for a Navy career.

Still, it was a little strange that I ended up at Annapolis, given my personality. But it had become a family tradition. My dad graduated from the Academy, as did my grandfather, and a couple of earlier ancestors did as well. I don't have any brothers or sisters, so it was pretty much dropped into my lap as a life goal. After I arrived at Annapolis, though, I really took to it.

But if we died, it was probably best that our families and friends never learn the precise circumstances. That way, they could imagine noble, painless deaths. The reality looked to be something different.

I said, "Talos, how much time?" I didn't want to rely on my wrist-computer. I wanted to hear Talos say it.

Talos said, "Missiles will arrive in a little over seven minutes."

"Okay."

The *sane* bridge-officers were in the brig. That was bad. They needed EVA suits. They needed to be released so that they could help defend the ship. We midshipmen didn't have any specific stations during general quarters, so I planned to go to the brig and see what was going on there.

I told the others my intention, and I stepped toward the ready-room's hatchway.

Lennox said, "I'm going with you."

As Lennox and I reached the hatch, we almost collided with my friend Lieutenant Waters. He was wearing an EVA suit, and he held his helmet in his hand. He stepped into the ready-room and put his helmet on the table, where the rest of us had placed ours. The helmets were uncomfortable, and we wanted to delay putting them on until we were sure we needed them to protect against possible decompression.

Waters said, "Astrid, this is one for the books. I

wanted to update you, since you were there when I carted Commander Rabinowitz away."

I said, "Are she and the others in the brig?"

Waters shook his head. "Not exactly. We left the cells unlocked. They're all in EVA suits, like us. If things blow over, they can stay there, and then hopefully return to their normal duties soon. If not, and if it looks like we're gonna be boarded, they'll grab shotguns and join up with us."

Talos announced, "Rotating ship to exhibit minimum silhouette. Launching sixty anti-missile drones."

The sixty drones represented all of the *Valley Forge*'s anti-missile drones. These drones were large craft, and they were armed with cannons and with Piranha missiles. Each of the drones was capable of launching four Piranhas. The missiles could separate into multiple independent warheads.

I asked Waters, "Where are you and your guys going to be?"

Waters said, "For us, it's dealer's choice during GQ. We don't generally take the Banshees out in these situations. Those are best used as attack craft. So our main purpose here is as backup turret gunners."

I said, "That's us, too. Back-up gunners."

Waters said, "Since Condition Zebra is in effect, the masters-at-arms are covering the reactors, engines, and missile platforms. Also, theoretically, the bridge. Talos will keep us posted on Captain Jefferson's activities. Right, Talos?"

Talos said, "Correct, Lieutenant Waters."

Waters continued, "Anyway, I checked the bridge when GQ was announced. Captain Jefferson was alone there. An MAA was leaving the area. Said the captain ordered him away."

"Above all else," I said, "Jefferson is still the captain. If we don't think he can serve, there are steps that can be taken. Otherwise, he stays the captain."

Waters sighed. "I know. We don't have any solid ground to stand on one way or the other. To relieve the captain might be bad. To allow him to continue might be bad. We're tiptoeing on the edge of a razor blade."

I said, "Maybe we should bring Talos in on this."

Waters nodded.

11

TALOS SPEAKS REGARDING MUTINIES

"Talos," I said, "can you give us a brief rundown on the law that applies to relieving a captain of duty?"

Talos said, "Relief of the commanding officer of a combat vessel may be initiated by no one other than the second in command."

I said, "I wonder who the second in command is now."

Talos said, "Logically, it cannot be any of the bridge officers now being confined, since, until the captain is determined unfit, all of his actions—including relieving the bridge officers of their duties—would be presumed lawful."

Waters said, "Maybe so. Talos, keep going."

Talos said, "Under United States Navy Regulations, the requirements are extensive and detailed. The circumstances must be most unusual and extraordinary. The situation must be obvious and clear, and the single conclusion must be that the retention of command will seriously and irretrievably compromise the public interests. Those are the main points."

Waters said, "Any procedural requirements?"

Talos said, "Whenever possible, the relief of the commanding officer must be approved in advance by the Department of the Navy."

Waters shook his head. "We don't have time for that. By the time we hear back from them, the battle will be over."

Talos said, "Then I suggest you transmit a message to them, stating what is intended, and explaining the urgency that prohibits awaiting approval."

I said, "What about mutiny?"

Talos said, "That is covered by the United States Code of Military Justice. It exists when two or more people refuse to obey orders, or do violence, or cause a disruption, with the intent to override lawful military authority."

Waters said, "That could cover almost anything. I think I'm guilty of that three or four times a day."

Talos said, "Penalties available for punishment of mutiny include death."

"All right," I said, "enough of this law-school stuff. What do we do?"

Waters said to me, "Do you see grounds for relieving Captain Jefferson of his command?"

I said, "According to my informal curbstone judgment, absolutely. According to what Talos has just said, no."

"That's my take on it, also," Waters said. "And that's why Rabinowitz and the others are in the brig, and that's why Rabinowitz hasn't replaced Captain Jefferson. If anything, those in the brig are guilty of a little insubordination."

In view of all that, I shelved thoughts of relieving the

captain of duty, or of mutiny. I said, "I'm thinking we don't have time for relieving the captain."

"Right," Waters said. "For us Marines, and maybe for you midshipmen, it seems best to focus on repelling boarders—assuming the Kerleegans don't simply blow the *Valley Forge* to pieces."

"You think they'll do that?" Lennox asked.

Waters said, "No. Once they have the upper hand—if for example we've exhausted our ordnance—they'll attempt to board us. At that point, if we beat them back, they will leave. Probably. At least, that's been their practice. Boiled down, they either get sick of losing people, or someone comes to rescue us."

Lennox asked Waters, "Do you know what overall course we're on now? Toward the enemy? Away? Zigzag?" She tapped her computer. "It looks to me as though we're in some kind of course correction that brings us closer to the enemy."

Waters laughed ironically. "I asked Commander Rabinowitz about that, and her view was the same as mine. At this point our course doesn't really matter. The enemy will stick with us. They have their optimum distance that they want keep between us and their bigger ships. Probably a thousand miles. We go closer, they move away. We move away, they follow. Precision doesn't matter. They simply need a staging area for delivery of their missiles, their interceptors, and their boarding parties."

Nash asked, "Can we expect help from other US ships?"

"Maybe," Waters said. "No other ships are in the vicinity, but I'm sure our GQ alarm went out to *everybody*." He looked at his watch. "I'm thinking if we can hold the enemy off for three hours, we'll have reinforcements. The ships themselves won't get here that fast, but I'm sure that even now they're burning propellant like mad. They'll launch a hundred Marlins, and you can bet your boots that'll put the fear of God into the Kerleegans."

I liked the sound of that.

Personally, I was hoping for a bunch of optimal conditions that would bring about the arrival of several hundred Marlins from other US ships, before the Kerleegans launched a single missile.

Wishful thinking? Yes, indeed. For one thing, from what Talos said, the Kerleegans had already launched missiles.

And three hours? That is a long, long time.

But it gets worse. I know Waters well enough to be aware that three hours was a time he pulled out of his hat. I believed that any reinforcements were likely to be ten or even twenty or thirty hours away. They weren't going to help us.

I usually think of our solar system as being pretty compact, in terms of the scope of outer space. But close distances in space can be enormous. As an example, Neptune's orbit has a diameter of well over five *billion* miles.

Our reinforcements could be many hours away—and in fact that would be their preferred distance. They could be running cold and untraceable. But if the Kerleegans lit their engines for even a few minutes, they would be trackable for days, because it would take so long for the heat to dissipate.

The US ships might pass by us days from now, when the *Valley Forge* is no more than a glowing wreckage, and still be hot on the trail of the Kerleegans.

It was not likely that any reinforcements would contact us by radio. We would gain no immediate benefit if they did, but they would give away their own position.

Then came another announcement by Talos over the ship-wide public-address channel (designated 1MC): "Gunners, watch your monitors. Incoming missiles and fighters two minutes out. Two hundred missiles. One hundred fighters."

12

HELL THROUGH THE VIEWPORT

The two-minute warning sent a chill through me.

Then Talos announced, "Shields up. Automatic angle-determination."

In the midst of that announcement, all lighting went to a dim setting, as power was diverted to the shields.

Talos then said, "Launching thermite flares."

The ready-room had monitors with video images from several cameras, but that wasn't what I wanted. I said, "I'm going to find a viewing port, to see what I can see."

Waters and Lennox went with me. Even though the ship was under Condition Zebra, which was a lockdown status during which most of the viewports were blocked, ports could easily be unblocked or re-blocked by hitting a switch at the port.

The three of us moved quickly toward a port-side corridor that led to the nearest viewing-port. This port was about two feet tall and eight feet wide.

I hit the switch, and the port's cover dropped down.

Through the viewport we could see a storm of the

thermite flares, which needed no oxygen source, and which burned bright and hot. These were not simply shot out randomly. Each flare had its own rocket engine, and they were guided by computer into optimum position. As seen through the port, these flares looked almost like a swarm of fireflies moving in all directions. The *Valley Forge* was equipped with four thousand of the flares, and this batch consisted of two thousand.

Many of the flares were now quite distant, several miles out. Others were near the ship.

Talos said, "Launching electronic jammers."

The jammers consisted of missiles with electronic jamming equipment, designed to interfere with the guidance systems of the enemy missiles. We could see the flames of our missiles as they moved out and dispersed.

Then we started seeing the detonations of the enemy missiles. All of those had heat-seeking sensors. Their job was to differentiate between different types of heat sources. At the same time, our flares were designed to mimic the principal target's heat signature.

It was a cat-and-mouse situation.

Our technology was superior, and the vast majority of enemy missiles failed. But the enemy's goal was really to overwhelm our defenses with sheer numbers. And obviously, even though we had a lot of things working for us, we had a finite supply of people and ordnance.

And almost immediately, some of the enemy missiles broke through.

The thermite flares actually lit up the area to a distance of a few hundred yards, and as those agile missiles slipped past the flares and the jammers, the antimissile drones went to work.

A lot of our defenses were technological marvels, but

those anti-missile drones were to me the most amazing. Each had a dozen rocket engines, which would be lit or dowsed according to whatever maneuvers were needed. They were the most fantastically maneuverable things ever. I mentioned that each of our drones carried four missiles, and you could pretty much bet the farm that each of those missiles would make contact with an enemy missile or fighter.

Talos announced, "Two hundred more enemy missiles incoming, to arrive in one minute."

We could take care of the first wave of two hundred enemy missiles. We might be able to deal with another wave, or maybe even two, especially if you consider the power of our drones.

The drones not only carried missiles, but they were also equipped with point-defense guns, which were multiple-barrel guns that could unleash ninety rounds per second. This was effective against missiles and fighters alike. If the enemy had strong shields, our drones could often maneuver to a place behind the enemy fighter. A half-second burst of twenty-five millimeter slugs into a fighter's rocket-nozzles usually destroyed the fighter.

It looked like a three-ring circus outside the ship, with enemy fighters and missiles maneuvering, and dueling with the drones. We could hear the gunfire from the turrets of the *Valley Forge.* We heard and felt the detonations of enemy missiles on the hull of our ship. And a couple of times I ducked, as enemy fighters swept across our view at close distances, probably ten or twenty feet from where we were standing.

It all had a nightmarish quality, and I thought it just might be what hell looks like.

I said, "Everyone seen enough?"

Waters and Lennox indicated in the affirmative.
I hit the switch, and the viewport was blocked again.

13

TOO MANY COOKS

Soon we were back in the ready-room. A horrendous cacophony came from the *Valley Forge*'s guns, and that was augmented by the racket of slugs and plasma balls hitting our ship. And we heard the continuing detonations on the hull of the *Valley Forge*, from the enemy missiles that made it through. Even though I knew of the strength of our hull and of our shields, I half-believed that the ship was being torn apart, and that I would soon be swept through some gaping opening, out into space, to die a horrible death by decompression.

The ready room was insulated, and normally it was as quiet as a graveyard. Ordinary sounds of the *Valley Forge*'s operation were completely masked when the hatches were closed. But the sounds of the battle that raged were easily heard within the ready-room. Though sound doesn't carry in space, the ship's structure and the atmosphere inside it had no problem bringing us the sounds that originated on the *Valley Forge*, in frightening clarity.

Our inertia dampeners weren't designed to absorb the

jarring and shaking of a ship under attack. One of the helmets fell from the table to the deck, and several times the ship shook so violently that I was barely able to remain on my feet.

I felt useless standing around in the midshipmen's ready-room. To be a soldier or sailor, trained for war, and to have the war playing out all around you without you yourself being involved—it's a miserable feeling. You feel like a shirker. Others are in the turrets, but you're just milling around and fretting.

At this point, Waters was in a good position to advise us. I asked him, "What can we be doing? We're all competent gunners. And pilots, for that matter."

Personally, I wanted to get out there in a Banshee. I wanted to do something, anything. What I *really* wanted to do was go after one of the enemy carriers, or one of the cruisers. I guess I was swept away by the idea of five midshipmen grabbing a bunch of Banshees and implementing a daring raid on the enemy ships. I couldn't really rationalize such a mission, but the appeal of the idea was almost overpowering.

Without waiting for a reply from Waters, I added, "I think we should man some of the Banshees—maybe engage the motherships."

Waters sighed.

I said, "Main question is whether we'll be needed as backup turret-gunners."

"Let me think," Waters said.

Then there was an enormous boom, which shook us all. It was likely the nearby crash of an enemy fighter into our hull.

Waters continued. "We have plenty of back-up gunners. The main problem is whether going out will be productive. The Banshees can hover near the *Valley Forge*, but that's not what they're designed for. If we try to hit their task force, odds are we won't make it in, and as for making it back to the *Valley Forge* . . . ."

I raised my eyebrows, waiting for a response.

Waters asked, "Who has charge of the midshipmen?"

"We're a special unit," I said. "We were placed directly under Commander Silver."

Waters said, "Let's see, and Silver is under Rabinowitz, and Rabinowitz is under Jefferson. Two of them are locked up, in theory at least. What are your standing orders during GQ?"

I said, "Defend the gun emplacements. Operate guns if necessary. Take all actions necessary to preserve the ship."

Waters said, "Okay, let's go. But let's focus on protecting the gun emplacements, and on trying to knock out their boarding craft, if we locate any."

I turned to the other midshipmen, and told them the plan. I added, "You're welcome to take a Banshee out, or you can stay here."

Nash said, "Cool, giving us two separate opportunities to die—in a Banshee, and later, on the *Valley Forge*. I'm in."

Lennox said, "Me, too."

I said, "Anyone else?"

Adler said, "Too many cooks'll spoil the broth. I don't want Astrid to waste valuable time watching out for me."

I quickly said, "Sounds good," because I didn't want him to change his mind. Adler's response was stated kiddingly, but he was serious in his analysis, and he was absolutely right. I was already having misgivings about more people going out. Waters and I would have been enough. But when *esprit de corps* kicks in, it's difficult for people to resist, even when it's foolhardy not to.

Nash said to Boyle, "Here's your chance to fly with champions. A joint Navy-Marines task force."

Boyle said, "No, I don't think so, Nash. I'm gonna keep Adler company. Depending on how things go, we might be needed as gunners, and at very least we can help with magazines and with replacing barrels."

Like Adler, Boyle was exercising good sense. I figured I'd give Nash and Lennox a chance to stay. I said, "Nash, maybe you want to stay here and help with the guns. You, too, Lennox."

Lennox was aware of what was going on. I knew she was committed to going out. I also knew that she was going to wait for Nash to respond, so that she wouldn't influence him.

But Nash breathed deeply and said, "Thanks, Astrid. I'm not changing course."

I nodded. I turned to Lennox and said, "Lennox?"

As I expected, she said, "Still in."

When you get down to it, there was no right or wrong course of action. I figured that staying on board offered a ninety-percent chance of survival for the next half-hour, at least. And I figured that with four of us going out in Banshees, it was likely that at least one of us wouldn't return. We didn't know what we were facing, and it might turn out to be an all-or-none situation. That is, there was a good chance that none of us would make it back.

Then Waters said, "Talos has programmed the Banshee weapons-systems with profiles of all known boarding craft used by the Kerleegans. We can focus on them."

That sounded fine by me.

The four of us bid farewell to Boyle and Adler. Nash's final words were, "Watch out for each other. And Adler, watch Boyle's six, will you?"

Adler said, "You got it, Nash. I've already picked out hiding places for both of us."

We all knew that there was nothing weaker about Boyle, but Nash was more worried about him, since he and Boyle had been friends since before the Academy.

Boyle took it in stride.

Everyone laughed at Adler's response. It wasn't a joyful laugh, really, but it was sincere. Overall, we were in good spirits—all things considered.

I said to Waters, "Which fighter bay?"

He said, "The port bay has the fittest ships. Also, the Banshees in the starboard bay are lacking missiles."

Waters, Lennox, Nash, and I threaded our way toward the port fighter-bay.

14

A DUBIOUS PLAN

After about twenty steps, Waters drew me near and said, "I'm gonna contact my people and recruit four more. My guys are always looking for a rumble, and they don't care about the odds. The way I look at it, if we add four guys, it increases the chances that you three midshipmen will all make it back."

I came to a halt, and so did Waters.

I said, "Let's tell Lennox and Nash that it's just you and me. We'll likely make it back after a little adventure."

Waters said, "That's not a bad idea. But no. First, staying here isn't going to be a Rocky Mountain Jamboree. And going out isn't a death sentence. Both situations are a little dicey. So we let each person follow his or her heart."

I said, "Okay, no change in plan."

Waters tapped his headset and looked at me for my approval of him contacting his people.

I said, "Go ahead."

So, Waters contacted the other Marines. He left three in their positions, and he brought in the four others, who were only too happy to leave their assignments and go out with us.

Waters, Nash, Lennox, and I continued to move toward the fighter bay. The other four Marines were to meet us there. As we neared the bay, I told Waters again I didn't like the idea of so many Marines coming with us.

He said he felt the same way, but this was war, and a lot of things happen in war that you wished didn't have to. There wasn't much else he *could* say. The decisions had already been made.

I said, "Amen." But I made a mental note to avoid this type of situation in the future, if possible. And if I lived that long.

The four of us reached the fighter bay, and then the four other Marines arrived. Most of the Marines on the *Valley Forge* were men in their late twenties and early thirties, and some of them had been Marines for more than a decade. They had seen it all, and what they didn't know about fighting probably wasn't worth knowing.

The racket of the battle didn't lessen. There was a continuing rapid bam-bam-bam from our gun emplacements, the sharp clatter of debris hitting the fuselage, and the pounding detonations of rockets on the *Valley Forge*'s hull.

Even though I was doubtful about the idea of eight of us taking part in what might turn out to be a fool's errand, I was glad that Nash was along. He had seemed jittery before, and I wanted to keep an eye on him. And I think he seemed calmer, knowing I was around.

As for me, I had a hollow feeling in the pit of my stomach. It was similar to the way I felt before a shooting match at the Academy, where I was a member of the intercollegiate shooting-team. It wasn't fear. It was an awareness that I needed to do my job, and that I couldn't afford to let my comrades down.

I had an unusual awareness of every part of my being. I was prepared to die, but at the same time I was confident that I would survive.

15

MABEL'S DREAM

There were two fighter-bays within the *Valley Forge*, with eight fighters in each bay. All of the Banshees had names painted on their sides—not pilot names, but nicknames for the particular Banshees. Most of the names weren't super-catchy, but they presumably had meaning for the guys who named them. These included *Hellfire*, *Stupid Cupid*, and *Quickdraw*.

All of the fighters had some appropriate image painted by the name. Some of the artwork was beautiful, and some of it was pathetic—as in all things, I suppose. I chose *Mabel's Dream*, and the accompanying image was that of a teddy bear. During the First World War, pilots sometimes affixed a teddy bear to a strut as a good-luck charm, so I figured that was the explanation.

I climbed onto a wing, and I heard Waters say, "*Mabel's Dream* is usually my bird."

I said, "Thought yours was *Lady Be Good*."

Waters was now standing a few feet away. He said, "She started being mean, so I ended our relationship. Go ahead and take *Mabel's Dream*. She's a good one."

I started to object, but Waters had already turned his back and was headed to a different Banshee.

I settled into the cockpit, and I strapped myself in. I tried to relax. It was then that I received a lesson on what Waters was all about. I knew he was married, but that was about all I knew of his life outside the Marines. Granted, I hadn't seen him at all after he left the Academy, but even so, I was surprised at how thin my knowledge of him was proving to be.

His cockpit had no fewer than four photographs of his wife, and what I assumed were his kids. I knew the woman was his wife, because one of the photographs was a wedding picture showing her and Waters. The kids were young, more like babies, and from their clothing, I figured they were both girls.

They all looked supremely happy. Waters looked like an ordinary guy, except with hair much shorter than most. His wife was gorgeous.

I thought of my fiancé, Joseph, and I hoped that someday he and I would be in photographs like these, and that they wouldn't be taped onto a bulkhead in a starship or onto the control panel of a Banshee, but instead would be in frames in a home somewhere.

Anyway, I suppose I didn't know much about Waters's life—his history, so to speak. But I knew what kind of a man he was—honest, forthright, trustworthy, courageous, helpful, caring. And besides, the cold facts that we think we know about others are often misleading, or downright false.

I was about to lower the canopy, when the sounds of battle tapered off to nothing. From that point on, all I heard were a few isolated sounds that were hard to place. I didn't know why that happened, but it struck me as ominous. The enemy might have silenced most of our guns. Or maybe they had terminated their missile attack to allow them to board us.

Talos opened the outer bay-door, leaving a forcefield in place to keep the bay compressed.

I kept listening, and still heard almost nothing. I waited till the last moment to lower my canopy.

One by one, we released our magnets, engaged the repulsors, and drifted through the ship-permeable forcefield. Soon all eight of us were in space, still near the *Valley Forge*. We didn't light our engines. We were relying on our reaction-control thrusters, which used compressed gas for maneuvering.

Outside, it was obvious that there was a major lull in the action. There were a half-dozen enemy fighters swirling around, and occasionally a missile would race in toward the *Valley Forge* from the distance. It was easier to see things on the Banshee's monitors than when looking through the canopy, because it was so dark out.

All of the *Valley Forge*'s exterior lights were off, and all ports, even the bridge's viewing port, were blocked. A few missiles contacted the ship, and the detonations provided a momentary bright light, but other than that, the *Valley Forge* looked completely black and was virtu ally invisible.

The general idea was that, in our Banshees, we would be mobile turrets. We would hang near the *Valley Forge*, and engage targets of our choice.

In theory, we were each on our own, which was fine by me. Maintaining a formation would have been impossible, and useless. None of us were really in a good position to take on any formal responsibilities to watch over each other, though I'm sure that most of us viewed ourselves as being responsible, in some way, for all of the others. I definitely tried to keep an eye on Nash and Lennox, especially on Nash. Lennox was actually a cool pilot, very smart, always alert, and she could take care of herself.

We set our sensors so that they were scanning mainly for the enemy boarding ships. This was good, since the break in the action was probably to allow the Kerleegans to attempt to board the *Valley Forge*.

There were several types of ships that the Kerleegans used when boarding one of our vessels. The worst, and most hated, form of boarding ship was one with effective boring tools that could create man-sized openings in the hull of a ship, usually causing decompression of significant portions. These boarding ships then shifted the boring tools away from the opening and released as many as a hundred enemy soldiers into the ship being attacked. A lot of us called those particular enemy ships Orphan Makers, or sometimes Grim Grinders. Those names never impressed me. Besides that, I didn't like giving nicknames to enemy equipment. It seemed like something the enemy would want us to do.

16

OUTSIDE THE VALLEY FORGE

As much as we disliked having our ships boarded, though, if I had to choose between boarding another ship and defending against boarders, I would rather be the defender. Repelling boarders is *always* less dangerous than being a member of the boarding party. If you're repelling boarders, you—in theory—know every nook and cranny of your ship. You can set up ambushes. You can plant extra weapons all over the ship. You can open trapdoors.

So, there are a number of effective measures that can be employed against boarders, but most of them have problems. Namely, certain solutions are equally effective against your friends and the enemy. You can't discharge directional anti-personnel mines, for instance, if your own people are in the line of fire of the mines.

The boarding of a ship, in which the boarders face resistance, is normally a chaotic undertaking, with aspects that are unpredictable and unique to the given boarding. The process is highly violent, and it involves unbridled ferocity on the parts of both the boarders and those repelling them.

And bloody? Yes, indeed, it might be the bloodiest aspect of space battle.

And regardless of which side might be favored, one of the principal goals of boarding an enemy ship is to strike terror into the hearts and souls of the defenders. The boarders are entering the enemy's *home.* And when they are beaten back, the boarders still have demonstrated to their enemies that they are not safe, even in their most inviolable places of refuge.

The other side of this coin is that a boarding normally takes place under extraordinary circumstances, which are often beyond the control of the personnel of the boarded ship. And once boarded, a ship's crew has no place to which retreat is possible. If necessary, they will fight to the last man, and on top of that they will usually, as a last resort, implement a self-destruct process, obliterating their own ship, even if that means killing their personnel who are alive at the time. Naturally, this is not always possible, but it can represent an effective way of taking your enemy with you when you leave the battle.

A footnote to this is that if you are part of a boarding party, and your side loses the fight, and you have the misfortune to be captured, you are likely to meet an extended and very painful end. The prevailing crew often takes matters into their own hands, and their leaders look the other way. This isn't the practice of our Navy. After all, most boarding parties are made up of ordinary soldiers or sailors, who have no say on anything, and who are following orders.

~

All eight of our Banshees were now outside of the *Valley Forge*. We had our scanners operating, and for a short time I saw nothing. Then I was picking up readings of enemy boarding craft affixed to the *Valley Forge*. We all had good communications with the other Banshee pilots, and with Talos.

I said, "Waters, do you see what I see?"

And Waters said, "It looks like four enemy boarding craft have attached themselves in single file along the bottom of the *Valley Forge*."

I said, "Right. Seems like this pause in the main attack is to allow the boarding. Did they knock out our ventral turrets? Why didn't we see the enemy craft on approach?"

Waters said, "Yes, I'm sure our ventrals are gone. We didn't see the boarding craft on approach, for the same reason we don't see them *now*."

I looked at my monitors again. They no longer showed the boarding ships.

Waters said, "Their stealth equipment is constantly adjusting for our changing sensor-frequencies. They're leaving us alone, because they don't want to give themselves away."

I said, "Waters, let's you, me, Lennox, and Nash drift down the starboard side, so that each one of us has an enemy boarding ship directly in front of us. We each launch our missiles, all six of them. We get out of the way, and four more Banshees take our places and do the same thing. We all get back to the fighter bay pronto. Thoughts?"

Waters said, "Let's do it." Then he added, "Everyone, if you're going to miss the targets, make sure you don't hit the *Valley Forge* in the process."

We implemented the plan. We were able to get into

the desired array quickly. There were four of us on a lower level. Fifty feet above each of us was another Banshee.

Waters, Lennox, Nash, and I moved down so that the boarding ships were straight in front of us. We were actually within the blast radius, but our shielding was adequate to protect us from the debris that would be thrown in our direction.

I glanced to the right and to the left. It was pitch-black out, and I couldn't see a thing, and our targeting sensors weren't reading the boarding vessels at all. It was as though the enemy ships weren't even there. We were relying solely on the images captured during that brief period when the frequency of our sensors revealed their positions.

I said to Waters, "See anything?"

"Negative."

"Why aren't they firing on us?"

Waters said, "They haven't got much in the way of defensive weapons in the first place. They definitely see us. But until we fire on them, they won't be sure *we* see *them*."

I said, "I'm thinking of throwing a spotlight on them, and launching Piranhas as soon as I can see the target and get it in my sights."

"Might be suicide. Might be genius. Do it."

I flipped on a spotlight. Nothing. I saw only the bottom of the *Valley Forge*. I panned the light back and forth. I could see nothing whatsoever out of the ordinary. I turned off the light.

Waters said, "Could they be gone?"

I said, "No. They're there. They're just well cloaked. I say we launch on spec, simultaneously."

"Count us down."

I said, "Nash, Lennox, sound good?"

They indicated that they liked the idea.

I said, "Three, two, one, launch."

On the word "launch," twenty-four Piranhas shot out toward the area beneath the *Valley Forge*. About half of the missiles missed their targets, but the other half connected beautifully with the boarding craft.

It was great to see, but we didn't have time to enjoy the sight. The four of us dropped down, and almost immediately our places were taken by the other four Banshees, which all launched missiles, and which did so with perfect accuracy—since their targets were in various states of glowing, molten wreckage, with no remaining stealth-protection.

We destroyed all four boarding ships, and in two cases, the boarding ship was torn loose from the *Valley Forge*. In the other two cases, what remained attached was meaningless rubble.

17

TRAGEDY IN THE TURRETS

All of the Banshees headed back to the fighter bay. I was thrilled that the eight of us returned unscathed. As we piloted our fighters into the bay, though, I was filled with apprehension. It was plain that the ventral turrets had been knocked out, but this was separate from the issue of whether we had lost any personnel. It could be that the guns were knocked out of commission, while the gunners remained unhurt. And it was possible that a gunner would be wounded, but not killed. I was worried, but hopeful.

On top of all that, my thought processes were not relaxed and coherent. I was riding on a distinct high as a result of our successful attack on the Kerleegan boarding craft.

I wanted to contact Talos for a report, but my mind was racing with so many thoughts that it was difficult for me even to concentrate on landing my Banshee. Waters and I were the last to reenter the *Valley Forge*. Within a second after enabling my magnets, fixing my Banshee to the deck of the bay, I glanced quickly around. Nash had been one of the first to land, and I saw him passing through the hatch that led to the port guns. All the others were still inside the bay.

Then I was on the comm line to Talos. I said, "Talos, update on our turrets, please."

Talos said, "Ma'am, I'm very sorry, but we lost both Boyle and Adler."

To be honest, that was the only information I was interested in. I was strangely callous about what else might have happened. I knew that any additional news would be bad, but to my mind it could not be as bad as what I had just heard. I said, "What else can you tell me?"

Talos said, "We lost all four ventral turrets. All four were entirely destroyed, and I pulled the guns, or what was left of them, and sealed the openings. The same applies to one port turret, two starboard turrets, and all four dorsal turrets."

"What happened with Adler and Boyle?"

"They replaced gunners who had been killed," Talos said, "and they in turn were killed. In all, we lost thirteen gunners."

"Which turrets were Adler and Boyle in?" I raised my canopy and started to exit my craft.

Talos said, "They were in starboard turrets three and four. Boyle was in three, Adler in four."

I said, "Anything else?"

"No, Ma'am, except that Midshipman Nash is moving rapidly from turret to turret. He probably is looking for Adler and Boyle. Do you want me to inform him as to what has happened?"

"No, don't do that. I'll do it, if I can reach him," I said. "When can we expect the next wave of attacks?"

"Based on the current location of the Kerleegan forces

and their normal methods, it will be at least fifteen minutes, and more likely twenty or so."

I said, "Keep me posted if you ever revise that."

"Yes, Ma'am."

~

I HAVEN'T BEEN alive forever, but one thing I've learned is that there is always someone who doesn't get the news, whatever that news may be—good, bad, important, trivial. In this case, the one who missed the news was Nash.

When we returned to the bay, Nash immediately departed through the hatch that ultimately led to the ready-room. I was sure he had gotten it into his mind that he would find Boyle there, or in one of the nearby port turrets. That was reasonable, because the port turrets were nearest to the ready-room, where we had left Adler and Boyle.

Nash and Boyle had known each other since grade school, went through high school together, fought together in the Navy, and later entered the Academy at the same time. The two had been roommates straight through the Academy.

In spite of his flirting a little with me, Nash had met a girl at the Academy, and he had told me several times he had expected that they would marry. Same thing with Boyle (different girl). I had met both of the women, and it all seemed like a good plan to me.

Of course, as I already mentioned, I was engaged myself, so it was comforting to have friends who were in the same situation. I even had pictured a triple wedding, involving Nash, Boyle, and me, and our future spouses. As usual, though, my imagination had parted from the reality that was to be. And then I started wondering whether Joseph would survive long enough to marry me.

I scrambled down off of my Banshee and ran over to Lennox. I grabbed her by the arm and pulled her along with me. We neared Waters, and I said to him, "Did you get the bad news?"

Waters said, "I'm afraid so."

I said, "Tell everybody who needs to know. Lennox and I are going to find Nash."

18

THE TWO GURNEYS

Lennox and I moved swiftly toward the turrets that had so ineffectively shielded my two friends. I was on the verge of tears, about Adler especially, since he had been so certain that the Navy would never put us students in a place where we might lose our lives. But it was also disappointing and sad that Boyle, a laid-back jokester, who I think really only wanted to loaf through this whole voyage, had lost his life as well. This loss was going to be terrible for Nash.

Lennox and I didn't say anything to each other. Lennox never talked much anyway, and besides, there really was nothing to say.

We jogged from corridor to corridor. Lennox was a few paces in front of me.

I said, "Talos, is any of the ship decompressed?"

Talos said, "No, Ma'am. The boarding craft never penetrated the hull, though they weakened it in a few places."

I said, "Hey, Lennox, let's get rid of our helmets."

Lennox came to a halt and immediately began

unsealing her helmet. She said, "Good idea, I've been dying inside this thing."

I smiled and nodded my head, "Same here."

We hooked our helmets to our waists, so that our hands would be free to hold our M90s. I should say that it was rare that we did not have our M90s and our sidearms with us. In fact, the Banshees had a special holder for the M90s, next to the pilot's seat.

We made a final turn to the left and were in the corridor that led to starboard-turrets three and four. Nearest to us was turret three, which had been manned by Boyle. The red light above the airlock was on, showing that the turret had suffered decompression. That by itself wasn't too unusual, since turrets are often penetrated during combat, and that's why all gunners wear EVA suits. In fact, sometimes the gunners will decompress the turret, if it looks like the turret will be breached. This avoids sudden decompression.

There was a gurney outside the turret, in the corridor. Nobody was around, other than Lennox and me. We moved in close to the airlock, since I assumed that medical personnel would be emerging soon with Boyle's remains. Down the corridor was another gurney, near the airlock that led to Adler's turret.

I said to Lennox, "Do you want to go down to Adler's turret? Nash is probably making a big U-turn, and he could show up at any time over there by Adler. Not sure if we should let him come down here."

Lennox said, "I'll do that," and she moved down the corridor at a trot.

Soon, the situation was simple. Lennox was by the gurney at Adler's turret, and I remained by Boyle's turret.

I dreaded seeing Boyle's remains, which, I believed, were probably thoroughly chewed up.

After about another minute, the airlock hatch opened, and two corpsmen were carrying Boyle's body out. Poor Boyle. It wasn't a pretty sight. I didn't see any blood or wounds, but an enormous section of Boyle's helmet had been torn off. The decompression killed him.

The corpsmen started lifting Boyle's body onto the gurney.

One of the corpsmen said, "Friend of yours?"

I said, "Yes, we're both midshipmen at the Academy. His name is Boyle."

The corpsman said, "Right, I see that." He tapped a clipboard that was resting on the gurney. "Raw deal for you middies. Come aboard for training, and then this."

I said, "What happened?"

"Half the turret's gone," the corpsman said. "Talos has already pulled what's left of the guns, and he's sealed off the opening."

I nodded and said, "Talos told me that."

The corpsman said, "There's a ton of debris in there, including some big pieces. I'm actually surprised Boyle's remains aren't torn up. Definitely a bad way to go, though." He extended his hand and said, "I'm Miles Gray. This is Hector Guzman."

I shook the hand of each of them and said, "Astrid Amundsen. Sorry to meet under these circumstances."

Guzman said, "We all have our jobs."

"That's so," I said. "I gather we lost all ventral turrets and all dorsal turrets, and a few others."

Gray said, "Right, eleven turrets, and along with them, thirteen gunners."

I said, "I wanted to say goodbye to Boyle here." I

patted Boyle two or three times on his stomach. "Also, Adler."

Gray picked up a clipboard from the gurney. He looked at it and then said, "Next one down, turret four." He pointed down the corridor, toward the other gurney, where two more corpsmen were loading Adler onto it.

I said, "I know. Lennox is down there. She's gonna stop Boyle's best friend from coming down here. She'll tell him what happened."

Guzman said, "We'll get Boyle's helmet off. We'll cover his head with the sheet. If his friend wants to see, he's welcome to. If it were me, I wouldn't want to."

I said, "I hear you." I said goodbye to Gray and Guzman, and I moved down the corridor.

The situation at Adler's turret was similar to that of Boyle's. The red light was on. The corpsmen were strapping Adler's body down, and Lennox was talking with them.

In the distance, Nash swung into the corridor.

19

LENNOX SAYS BOYLE IS DEAD

Lennox raised her arm, and Nash moved quickly toward her. When he arrived, Lennox patted Nash's helmet, and he removed it, with Lennox's help.

I was now about fifty feet from them, and I could hear their voices, in muffled tones. I couldn't make anything out.

Lennox moved to place herself between Nash and the gurney that held Boyle.

They spoke a little more. Nash moved toward Lennox. She backed up a little, and they exchanged a few more words.

Then, unexpectedly, Nash grabbed Lennox's shoulders and threw her roughly aside, and he started to jog towards me.

But Lennox recovered in no time, and Nash was running slowly, with hesitation. Lennox caught up with Nash and threw her arms around his waist.

At this time, I was only twenty feet from the two of them.

Nash looked at me, and he stopped resisting.

Lennox released him from her hold.

Nash remained standing where he was, and he said, "Lennox says Boyle is dead. Is that true?"

I said, "Nash, I'm so sorry."

Lennox stepped around Nash so that she could stand beside me.

Nash looked utterly defeated. His shoulders slumped, and he stared at the deck and shook his head.

Lennox and I looked at each other and shrugged slightly.

Then Nash seemed to recover a little, and he nodded a few times. He looked at me and asked, "Boyle is being taken care of?"

I said, "Yes, he is, Nash."

Nash said, "Let's check on Adler. Maybe he's okay."

Lennox said, "Nash, he's not."

"But he might be," Nash said. "Let's go check on him."

Neither Lennox nor I replied.

The three of us walked back to Adler's gurney. His helmet was on the gurney by his feet. The corpsmen were about to wheel him away, but they stopped when they saw us.

Nash said to the corpsmen, "We need to check on Adler. I think he's still alive."

The corpsmen looked quickly at Lennox and me.

Lennox said, "Right, we need to make sure." She was just being kind. Lennox and I were already sure.

I wasn't all that interested in getting a closer look.

One of the corpsmen pulled the sheet back off Adler, down to his thighs.

"I don't see any wounds," Nash said. "He's alive all right. He's knocked out. That's all that's wrong."

One of the corpsmen said, "No, we checked and double checked, and triple checked. We checked brain activity and heart, everything."

Nash said, "But he wasn't even hit."

At this point, the corpsmen must have understood that Nash wasn't acting rationally. My own view was that Nash was using Adler as a test case. If Adler were still alive, then Boyle was also alive.

I glanced behind us, and I saw that the corpsmen with Boyle were not moving. Likely, they knew what was going on and figured they would wait until the situation resolved itself.

With his voice full of understanding and compassion, the corpsman said to Nash, "This happens sometimes. The gunner sustains fatal wounds, maybe many. The suit seals up the small openings on its own. Little if any blood makes it outside the suit. In this case Adler took a lot of hits. Sad to see this happen to you guys."

Nash looked bewildered.

The corpsman pointed to several places on Adler's suit. "See? Here, and here, and here, and down there. All in places your armor plates don't cover. And then probably fifty hits where the plates worked."

Nash's voice was hoarse when he said, simply, "I see."

"Most of the hits," the corpsman said, "were from tiny fragments spraying in through openings in the turret. You know, from collisions of the enemy missiles and fighters."

I said, "Makes me wonder whether we need better plates, or more of them."

The corpsman said, "You do. Here the Kerleegans penetrated the turret's shielding, and its armor. That's unusual. But when they want to get rid of a turret, they keep at it, to the point of suicide. They'll send missile after missile, to kind of soften things up. Then if necessary they'll crash fifteen or twenty fighters into a turret. It's hard to withstand that type of attack."

I said, "Right, hard." I patted Adler twice on the stomach, following the little tradition I had started with Boyle.

Lennox and Nash did the same.

We shook hands with the corpsmen as best we could with our bulky gloves, and said farewell.

I said to Nash and Lennox, "Let's go this way," as I gestured toward the stern. We moved out on a route that would take us away from Boyle.

I turned briefly to Gray and Guzman, who were now starting to wheel Boyle away.

I raised my arm in thanks, and they saluted.

20

BACK IN THE READY-ROOM

Soon, we were back in the ready-room. The eight Marines were there, I suppose just waiting for the next assault on the *Valley Forge.* All eight of them were armed with shotguns, so they all expected the next action to take place on board the ship.

Lennox, Nash, and I sat at one of the tables. Nash was across from Lennox and me.

Waters and the other Marines kept their distance. They didn't say anything.

Nash was silent, seemingly lost in thought. His hands were on his lap, and his face bore a slightly stern expression.

Nash looked up at Lennox and me, but his expression hardly changed.

I said, "You all right, Nash?"

Nash said, softly, almost as though he were in a daze, "Sure. Why wouldn't I be?"

I sighed, and I said, "Well . . . Boyle."

Nash smiled subtly and said, "Boyle?" He paused, then repeated himself. "Boyle?" He tapped the table with his finger, then reached to his throat and pulled up on a slender chain. Affixed to the chain was a pendant, in the form of a little gold medal. Nash grabbed the medal in his right hand and balled the hand into a fist.

I winced as Nash jerked his hand outward forcefully.

The chain snapped.

Nash held his hand out in front of him and opened it. He turned his hand, and the medal fell to the table.

I said, "Nash, what is that?"

He said, "It's Our Lady of Mount Carmel. You know, Saint Mary. Patron saint of sailors. Boyle gave it to me."

I asked, "That's good, right?"

"Oh, I don't think so," Nash said. "I gave one to Boyle, too. It didn't do him any good, did it?"

"Nash," I said, "a medal doesn't *protect* you. It *reminds* you."

"I don't want it."

"You need to keep it, Nash."

Nash touched the pendant with his index finger. He spoke slowly and calmly. "What do I need *this* for? It's only a little piece of metal."

Nash swiped his hand across the table, shoving the medal off the table and onto the floor. Waters stepped over to the medal and picked it up.

No point in arguing with Nash. I nodded and said, "Just metal."

Nash took a deep breath, and still speaking slowly, he said, "I've been thinking, Astrid. Our group actually will be better without him. Like you always say, it's not *how many*, it's *who*. Right?"

I nodded hesitantly. "Right, Nash."

"And," Nash said, "Boyle was always creating problems. *Can I borrow this, Nash?* Or *Nash, can I borrow that? You don't need it.* All the time, Astrid." Nash's voice wavered a little. "Lots of times he took my stuff without even asking. And he was *always* talking, saying the stupidest things. And Astrid, he just would never shut up. Honestly, we're better off without him, you know? You can understand how I feel, right?"

I looked over at Lennox. Her eyes were red, and tears were streaming down her cheeks.

I placed the palm of my hand flat on the tabletop and slid it slowly outward toward Nash. I said, "Nash, I understand *exactly* how you feel. I feel the same way. So does Lennox."

Nash placed both of his hands over his face and wept softly.

~

Nash managed to pull himself together somewhat, after many consoling remarks from Lennox. I can't remember exactly what she said, but it was lovely to listen to her. She said that as long as we remembered Boyle, he would still be alive. She said that when we got back to Annapolis, we would have a little ceremony celebrating Boyle's life. She said that Boyle had often told her that he admired Nathan Hale and his sentiment that he regretted having only one life to lose for his country.

Whether that last part was true or not, Lennox managed to bring Nash to a point where he could begin to make more sense of Boyle's death.

And I actually felt a weight being lifted from me, since I realized that I was no more responsible for Nash than Lennox was. And more generally, I saw that the world of the midshipmen did not revolve around me. The three of us were equals. There was nothing special about me, except in my mind.

I said, "Talos, what's going on now? We haven't had any updates from you."

Talos said, "There has been nothing to report. I should have further information soon, though. The Kerleegans are not going to stay uninvolved much longer."

I asked, "What's happening on the bridge?"

"Captain Jefferson is alone there," Talos said. "He is studying monitors and has been doing so ever since the other bridge officers were taken away."

21

DAMAGE REPORT

I was glad that we were experiencing this brief respite in the battle. It allowed us to recover somewhat from the ugly events so far, and to do a little planning for what was to come. I said, "Talos, how much damage have we done to the enemy, when compared to the damage they've inflicted on us?"

Talos said, "During the principal conflict, we launched four hundred Coffin Nails, and two hundred Piranhas. Our supply of those missiles is now exhausted, except for the Piranhas now mounted to some of the Banshees in the port bay."

Lennox interrupted. "How is that the case regarding the Banshees?"

Talos said, "A weapons crew is now in the process of rearming four of the Banshees in the port bay with a full complement of six missiles on each. Those are the only remaining Piranhas."

Lennox nodded.

Talos continued. "We also launched one hundred

thirty-two Marlins, and sixty drones. Our missiles destroyed hundreds of enemy missiles and fighter craft."

I wanted to learn how effective our guns had been. I asked, "And what about our turrets?"

"Our gunfire destroyed dozens of enemy craft," Talos said. "Additionally, the enemy lost another hundred craft through suicide crashes on the turrets, and many of their missiles detonated on the hull or turrets."

I said, "From what you're saying, both sides inflicted approximately equal damage on each other, as to weapons and equipment."

Talos said, "So far, that is true."

Waters cleared his throat and looked around at the others in the ready-room. He asked, "And we lost thirteen crew members?"

"Correct," Talos said evenly.

It seemed to me that Talos's answer to Waters was completely without sympathy. Yet Talos had said he was sorry when he told me that Adler and Boyle had been killed. Of course, it would be absurd to think that Talos experienced genuine feelings. Nonetheless, I found it intriguing that Talos expressed sadness when he was speaking of two specific people, whom he knew to be important to me and the other midshipmen.

That was similar to the ways *people* tend to view calamities. If we hear that two hundred people died because of an earthquake, we say, "That's unfortunate," but generally we move on without difficulty. But if we learn that a parent or sibling died on account of some natural disaster, it turns our whole world around.

Waters continued to address Talos. "How many Kerleegans have been killed?"

"Including those on boarding craft," Talos said, "well over a thousand."

Waters said, "Too bad they don't seem to care much about losing personnel."

Talos said, "One other thing to bear in mind is the fact that significant damage has been done to the *Valley Forge*. And we have expended almost all of our missiles. We have twenty-eight Marlins remaining and then that handful of Piranhas."

"Talos," I asked, "what tactics do you recommend?"

"The best advice," Talos said, "is to keep doing what you are doing. You must be prepared for boarding, and make the fight as bloody for them as you possibly can. The Kerleegans tend to persist far beyond what most nations would find reasonable. They will lose thousands of soldiers to gain a minor victory. They value the lives of their soldiers very little, but at some point they may decide that further losses are not worth sustaining. Their calculations on such matters are entirely unaffected by emotion."

Waters said, "All right. That's consistent with what we've heard before."

"Yes," Talos said. "This is all based on what we have learned from prior experiences in this war. And even if they should annihilate everyone on board—and there is an excellent chance that they will do that—you must make them pay as dearly as possible. Down the line, this may make them more reluctant in future boarding endeavors."

No one said anything. I think we all were displeased with the rather downbeat assessment that Talos provided.

Although Waters had been participating actively in the discussion with Talos, the other seven Marines had simply listened stoically, not reacting in the least to anything that Talos was saying. The same applied to Nash and Lennox. I'm sure that the deaths of Adler and Boyle had made real the idea that none of us were safe.

I looked at Nash. He now was nodding his head, almost as though he had experienced an epiphany. I was glad that he wasn't drifting inward with his thought patterns. I hoped that he was reestablishing a semblance of normalcy, at least for the time being, until after our crisis passed.

22

NASH'S QUESTION

Nash cleared his throat and said, "Other than the generalized 'kill as many as you can,' what *specific* strategies can you offer?"

Talos said, "These are subjective things, but I will be as specific as possible. Some of these might require orders from—from *someone.* All right. First of all, it is crucial that all strategies and tactics be evaluated independent of Captain Jefferson. Secondly, eleven of our original sixteen turrets are now out. I would migrate shielding from non-critical areas in order to double or even triple the shielding at the remaining guns. Thirdly, I would use this ready-room as a base of operations. Enemy ships will likely concentrate on the forward areas of the ship. Those are less protected than the stern, which contains the engines and reactors and the remaining Marlins."

Then there was silence.

Talos added, "The crew is now operating under standing orders relating to General Quarters. Someone has to assume effective control of the ship and give whatever additional orders may be necessary."

Waters said, "That situation is a little iffy. The highest-ranking officers under Jefferson are in the brig. Next highest are a bunch of lieutenants."

"Well," I said, "those guys are presumably directing their people. But we do need some kind of overall plan."

Talos said, "Someone needs to be the commanding officer. One last point. Careful consideration must be given to the deployment of the remaining Marlins. I would say use them on the boarding craft. But, to state the obvious, when they're gone, they're gone. In any event, you want to make the boarding a miserable process for them. Let them board in large numbers, and destroy them by the hundreds, via methods of your choosing. I think that covers my advice."

I said, "Okay, thanks for your contribution here."

"Also," Talos said, "I want to thank Midshipman Nash for asking. I don't often have the chance to act as a captain might. Again, these are all subjective ideas. Be directed by the seat of your pants."

"All right, then," Nash said.

Waters said, "Talos, you don't need any formal authorization to divert extra shielding to the remaining guns, so go ahead and do that. Unless and until Captain Jefferson gives further orders, or we get a different commanding officer in place, we'll be guided by common sense. We'll protect the ship to the extent of our capabilities, by every means at our disposal."

Talos said, "All right, I'm now strengthening the shielding at the remaining guns."

All was quiet.

Then Talos said, "Enemy drones are drawing near. These are surveillance drones only. No weapons to speak of. The drones will report back to the Kerleegans, and they will believe that the coast is clear for their boarding."

Waters said, "Makes sense."

Talos said, "Eight Kerleegan boarding craft are now on course toward the *Valley Forge*. They are escorted by thirty interceptors."

Everyone grew silent. As often happened during quiet times, my thoughts drifted to Joseph. He always said he hoped that the two of us would someday be assigned to the same ship. It's a two-edged sword. If a husband and wife are assigned to the same ship, it may happen that both die. That has actually occurred more than once. The chances of that are greatly lessened if they serve on different ships.

Nonetheless, I fervently wished that Joseph were with me, even though the future looked bleak. I believed that somehow he would find a way out. Also, I felt as though I was out of my depth in some of the situations I was facing. And I believed that my decisions might be more thoughtful and mature if he were around to perhaps provide a little guidance.

Talos said, "Captain Jefferson is now vacating the bridge."

This brought me abruptly out of my contemplations. I said, "Where is he heading?"

Talos said, "Unclear at this time. His route, however, is in the direction of the port fighter-bay, in which your group landed a little while ago."

I shook my head and said softly, "Oh, wonderful. What next?"

As I waited for clarification on the captain's destination, I experienced a few insights. Usually I thought of a battle as an all-out fight between two groups of soldiers.

There are some tactics, determined by the leaders. Do we flank the enemy? Do we engage in a frontal assault? That type of thing. The enemies fight, and one side wins. That determines a battle, and a war is made up of many battles. Neat, clear, organized.

In reality, war is nothing like that. War is actually troops that are too tired to march to the battle, and too hungry or sick to fight in it. It's equipment that is broken or poorly designed. It's missiles that won't fire, or which go off course, and which maybe circle back and destroy you. It's booby-trapped war souvenirs. It's unpopular squad-leaders getting fragged by their own men.

The miracle isn't that your side won, it's more that your forces were even able to find the enemy they're supposed to fight—and sometimes they can't even do *that*. Incompetency is everywhere. The shambolic muddle of war exists in the actual fighting, but even more so, it's seen in what goes on behind the scenes.

I knew that these things were features of war, but now, for the first time, it dawned on me that these types of things were the very *essence* of war.

It our case, we had a captain who had gone off his rocker, and who was now wandering around the ship, maybe looking for a golden fleece. And the three next in command were in the brig, but even that had its own wrinkles, since the cells weren't locked.

Perhaps weirdest of all, we midshipmen were acting like we knew what we were doing, when we were actually trainees. And then there was my firm belief that the Department of Defense had sent us out here like a worm on a hook. We were simply bait, unprotected and forlorn.

I was pulled out of my thoughts by Talos.

"Captain Jefferson is entering the fighter bay," Talos said.

"Same bay we landed in?" I asked.

"Yes."

I didn't wait around to talk. I grabbed my helmet and rushed off toward the bay.

23

JEFFERSON ON THE LOOSE

I made it to the bay, followed by Lennox and Nash. Once again, it seemed as though I were leading them. I hadn't intended it that way. I think I was a little more rash and impulsive, so that made me act first.

Jefferson was seating himself in a Banshee, one called *Pilgrim's Progress*. He turned his head to look back at the raised canopy, then he faced forward and began to strap himself in.

I was about eighty feet from him, and I yelled out, "Captain Jefferson!" I sprinted toward him.

Jefferson stopped cold what he was doing, and he said, "Amundsen, did you hear what Talos is saying?"

I reached the side of his interceptor, and I was breathing hard. I said, "You mean about the drones and the boarding ships and the interceptors?"

Jefferson said, "Yes, precisely. I don't know where everybody else is. They should all be here by now. But I'm glad to see the three of you here."

I glanced to my side. Lennox and Nash were standing

next to me. I said, "Yes, Captain, we're here." And now my heart was truly in my boots. I believed that if we left there with Captain Jefferson, none of us would return. I sensed doom, and why wouldn't I?

My mind flashed forward to what I was sure was going to happen. I pictured someone asking Waters, in a few days, *What happened to Jefferson and those three midshipmen?* And in my mind's eye, I saw Waters drawing his hand across his throat.

Anyway, Jefferson said, "We need to meet force with force. Are you joining me? It'll be dangerous. This is strictly an all-volunteer mission."

My instinct was to say, "Are you *insane*? There's no way any of us are going with you!"

But for some unknown reason, what I actually said was, "You don't need to ask. You're our captain. Where you go, we go." Then I added, "I should speak for myself. Nash and Lennox may have other ideas."

Lennox said, "I'm in, Captain. You too, right, Nash?"

Nash said, "I wouldn't miss it for the world."

So, it looked like Nash had now recovered, at least for the moment. Or maybe he simply had a death wish. I was disappointed that Lennox had actively encouraged Nash, but at this point I simply wanted to get on with it.

Captain Jefferson looked at my two companions. He nodded and said, "Lennox and Nash." He looked at me for a moment and then said, "Good job by the three of you, earlier. I'm not surprised to see you three here. I was sorry to lose Adler and Boyle."

I almost fainted when he mentioned the names of Adler and Boyle, and doubly so when it became clear he was aware that Adler and Boyle were gone. I wondered whether Jefferson's psychosis—I was still certain he was gone—somehow gave him a special ability to remember names and facts.

I said, "Captain Jefferson, what tactics do you recommend?"

Jefferson said, "We ignore the scouting drones. Eight Kerleegan boarding craft are approaching. Our goal is to knock out all of them. But I'm a realist, Amundsen. Maybe we'll only get five or six of them. Our computers will do most of the work. Ultimately, we'll each launch two volleys of three missiles. The computers will coordinate and select the best target for each of us. We launch missiles as soon as we get locks. Then we wait for new locks and launch again. That should take care of all eight boarding craft. Then we loop back toward this bay. Their fighters will come after us with missiles. We launch countermeasures on my say-so. That's all."

This sounded to me like a plan that was doomed not just to failure, but to abject, abysmal failure. Eight boarding craft and thirty interceptors, against our four Banshees, didn't seem favorable. And the fact that Jefferson had been willing to take the enemy on by himself wasn't exactly an endorsement of his sanity or judgment.

Yet Jefferson's plan appealed to me, I think because of its epic simplicity. We fly out, fire our missiles at the boarding craft, and defend against the enemy missiles by deploying anti-missile countermeasures. Easy. Also, Captain Jefferson's confidence, whether it arose out of insanity or not, was contagious.

But I *was* experiencing conflicting feelings. On the one hand, I felt as though I were a mountaineer scaling

Mount Nobility. On the other hand, it seemed as though I were a certifiable psychotic on a toboggan ride down Madness Mountain.

24

NO HELMETS

I would have loved to have more time to think things over, but this situation wouldn't allow it. Sure, I had misgivings, but I plowed them under. I said to Jefferson, "Sounds good. Lead the way. Oh—aren't you going to wear a helmet?"

"No," Jefferson said. "I'm just going to trust *this*." He reached downward out of the cockpit with his left arm and rapped the fuselage of the Banshee. "Solid as Gibraltar. I don't need the heads-up display, either. I'll rely on the cockpit display. What about you?"

Ideally, helmets would be a given. Otherwise, if your cockpit is breached, then you're dead, period. Also, built into the helmets was a sophisticated heads-up display that integrated a great deal of information, not the least of which were targeting data and audible alerts. Yes, you can fly a mission without the HUD, but then you are glancing every which way inside the cockpit, and that impairs your effectiveness.

Nonetheless, I said, "Well—same here."

What else could I say? *If it's all the same to you*

Captain, I'm afraid of decompression. I'm going to wear a helmet.

I don't think so. It was like peer pressure, even though Jefferson and I weren't peers.

Lennox and Nash were still beside me. They both nodded. They weren't going to wear helmets either. I think we all felt that we were part of something bigger, when Jefferson invited us along. Sure, we were part of the Navy, and the Navy is big. But Jefferson was our captain, and we were following him into battle. Here was a guy who was out in front of us, as a leader should be. And you don't always see that, even in the Navy. So, *of course* we went with him. We felt special—or at least *I* did.

Jefferson thumped his chest three times with his right hand and said, "I'm proud to be flying with the three of you. I can't tell you how good it feels to have the support of members of my crew."

I slapped the side of Jefferson's Banshee three times, and I said, "Fair winds and happy landings, Captain. *Semper fortis.*"

Jefferson smiled solemnly and said, "*Semper fortis.*"

Nash and Lennox repeated the words back to Jefferson and, as I had done, slapped his Banshee three times.

Then the three of us headed toward our interceptors.

When I was almost to my Banshee, Waters and a couple more Marines arrived. Waters ran up to me and asked, quietly, "Astrid, what do you think you're doing?"

I smiled weakly and said, "Dying, I'm pretty sure. Just

go back to the ready-room, and make sure you get everybody to pray for us."

Waters said, "Astrid, if you're going, take this." He handed me Nash's Saint Mary medal. He said, "Don't give it to Nash. I don't know how he'd react. When you get back here—and make sure you do—you can tell him you had it with you."

I said, "Better idea: I'm gonna give it to Jefferson."

Waters said, "Do it." He patted my shoulder and said, "Fair winds, my sister."

I said, "Gracias, fair winds, my brother," and Waters and the other Marines departed, probably in a state of high distress.

I ran to Jefferson's Banshee and jumped up onto the wing.

Jefferson had been waiting for me to finish with Waters, and his canopy was still open. I handed the medal to Jefferson, saying, "Lieutenant Waters wanted you to have this. It's Mary, patron saint of sailors."

Jefferson took the medal. He looked at me and said, "*Un beau geste*." He crossed himself, and then he kissed the medal and said, "Thank you, Astrid."

I said, "Let's all make it back in one piece."

Jefferson nodded and said, "I'll see you back here, soon."

I said, "Count on it," and I was off to my Banshee.

To be honest, though, I felt a little like Joan of Arc on her way to be burned at the stake.

25

NO FOOL LIKE AN OLD FOOL, EXCEPT MAYBE THREE YOUNG FOOLS

Within a half-minute, all four of us had released our magnets and were using our reaction-control thrusters to maneuver out of the bay.

We all pointed our Banshees in the direction of the enemy and remained in a row, each about fifty feet from the next.

Jefferson said, "Light your engines, then match my speed."

My own engines lit with a roar accompanied by a cyclonic howl.

We flew next to each other, in a row, toward the enemy, with an acceleration of five Gs. In front of us was nothing but the purest blackness, except for the abundant stars. Our engines were burning brightly, though, and the flames from the nozzles dimly illuminated the exteriors of all of our Banshees.

My monitors showed the enemy drones as they neared the *Valley Forge*. We zipped past them without ceremony. I could also see the eight boarding craft on my screen, and the thirty interceptors, all marked with little icons.

We were moving at high speed toward the enemy, and the enemy was coming rapidly toward us.

My targeting system searched for a lock, and it coordinated with the computers on the other fighters so that we each would launch at a different boarding ship.

I knew that all of the locks would occur simultaneously, or nearly so. The Piranhas have their own countermeasures, including chaff and thermite flares, and I figured that once we launched, at least *some* of our missiles would get through.

And there it was: a high-pitched, unmistakable tone. And my monitor's sights were directly over one of the boarding craft.

Within a second of my hearing the tone, I launched three missiles, and for a second I watched the ominous flames gushing from their engines as they shot into the blackness. I hoped that the countermeasures of the Piranhas would also help us in our fighters. We were certainly close enough to them. Before I looked away, I saw the other nine missiles shooting out from the Banshees of my teammates.

Now I was hoping for the rapid targeting of the remaining four boarding craft. Sure enough, almost immediately the sharp tone sounded again, signifying another lock, and my second volley of three missiles was off, as were those of the other three Banshees.

With that, we all yanked back on our control wheels, and our Banshees swept upward as we each executed a wingover, using our RCS thrusters, as well as our adjustable engine-nozzles, to change our vectors. The result was a reversal of direction at a position about a half mile above our earlier trajectories.

So far, so good. I studied the monitor to see the effects of our attack. Plainly all twenty-four missiles had released countermeasures, since the images on the screen showed thousands of specks. And then, to my gratification, four of the icons, representing boarding craft, disappeared from the screens.

And then, to my amazement, four more of the icons disappeared. We had destroyed all eight of the enemy boarding craft. Yes, the Kerleegans would likely send more, but I hollered loudly to myself in my joy at our complete victory against these eight. It was very unlike me to do that, but deep down I felt happy that I had accomplished something, and also I felt good that Captain Jefferson's mission had been accomplished.

Then I realized that I wasn't simply yelling to myself. The others heard me and said things like, "Yeah! We did it, Amundsen!"

In my book, the mission was a success. But it still remained doubtful that we would make it back alive. We weren't out of trouble. All thirty of the Kerleegan escort craft were after us. They weren't quite as fast as us, and they were well behind us. But if they launched missiles, it would be a tricky situation. We would have to rely mainly on our own countermeasures.

Sure enough, the Kerleegan interceptors began launching missiles. Each enemy fighter carried four missiles. If they launched all of them, there would be one hundred and twenty missiles streaking after Jefferson, Lennox, Nash, and me.

When there were about thirty missiles pursuing us,

Jefferson said, "Midshipman Amundsen, countermeasures."

26

OUT OF OUR WAY! WE'RE U.S. NAVY PILOTS!

I released all my countermeasures. This included hundreds of thermite flares, as well as chaff to interfere with targeting. Halfway through the process, I saw on my monitors the explosions of many missiles, which had detonated on the thermite flares. Several missiles shot wildly in different directions, because of the chaff's interference with their guidance systems.

Another storm of enemy missiles came at us. Jefferson said, "Midshipman Lennox, countermeasures." Then, almost immediately, Jefferson added, "Midshipman Nash, countermeasures."

I could see on my rearview video-display a spectacular array of thermite flares and detonations of missiles.

Jefferson said, "Launching countermeasures," and he released his.

The last of the enemy missiles had been launched, and my monitors showed that the enemy fighter-escort, having exhausted their missiles, had peeled back.

Our countermeasures were doing their job. The detonations of enemy missiles were taking place by the dozen, and I wondered how many missiles would make it through.

I asked my Banshee's computer, "How many enemy missiles remain?"

And my computer replied, "Twenty-four remain viable."

Jefferson said, "We're almost home. Twenty-four missiles to beat. If you have any extra juice, use it now."

I don't know about the others, but I already was using all available engine-thrust, supplemented slightly by my RCS thrusters. I also jettisoned about two hundred pounds of inert kinetic slugs, and I assume the others had done the same. But my fighter was falling behind the others.

Jefferson said, "All of you, light your cockpit lights. I want to see who I'm flying with."

Tactically that was generally a poor idea. Under the circumstances it was probably okay, but it was a little ostentatious. It reminded me of the flamboyant General George A. Custer, and we all know how *he* ended up. Nonetheless, I liked the idea so much that I lit my interior lights without hesitation.

The others lit theirs, too, and it was comforting to be able to see them, though they were growing more distant in front of me.

Then a voice from the Valley Forge broke in. "Waters here, to Captain Jefferson. Excuse the interruption. We're launching the rest of the Marlins. Happy landings."

"Good show, Lieutenant Waters," Captain Jefferson said. "We'll see you soon."

Then I could see, in front of us, the rocket blasts of our remaining twenty-eight Marlins. Waters had done the common-sense thing and launched Marlins in an effort to facilitate our escape, or to put it more bluntly, to save our hides.

The flames of the rocket engines of the Marlins, angling toward us in the blackness, were a dramatic sight. They came almost directly at us. Of course, they could distinguish between friends and foes, and they shot right past us.

More detonations!

A few moments later, Jefferson said, "We've still got two live ones remaining. Everyone under the *Forge*!"

I loved to hear Jefferson call our ship the *Forge*.

Jefferson said, "Lighting all lights."

I followed suit, as did Lennox and Nash. We had our navigation lights on, also our anti-collision beacons, our formation lights, our floodlights, and our spotlights. If it could be made to glow, we lit it. Yes, it was arrogant of us, and maybe even a little imperious, but I was thinking, *Get out of our way! We're US Navy pilots!* And I don't think I had ever felt more proud than I did at that moment.

The four of us shot under the *Forge*, all of us doing about five miles per second, and our mothership disappeared behind us almost immediately.

But I was falling farther behind, and the enemy missiles were closing the gap.

27

CAPTAIN, SUGGESTIONS?

My Banshee was now about a hundred yards behind the others, and the enemy missiles were about the same distance behind me. I said to Jefferson, "Captain, suggestions?"

Jefferson said, "Yes, Amundsen. Hold her straight and normal."

Jefferson evidently had power in reserve, and he leaped out even further in front of me and the others.

Then he said, "Lennox! Nash! Excellent work. Get back to the *Forge*."

I saw the other two midshipmen veer back around, and I was thankful beyond words that they, at least, had made it through this difficult and dangerous mission.

Now Jefferson was far in front of me. I studied my monitors, wondering how he intended to help me out of this fix.

The Kerleegan missiles continued to gain on me.

Then events unfolded with great rapidity. Jefferson said, "Cutting engines and flipping." Then he used his RCS thrusters and reversed direction, to aim his ship back in my general direction. Though his Banshee was pointed toward me, his momentum was carrying him in the same direction in which I was moving.

My ship closed in on him quickly, as did the missiles, which were now about forty yards behind me.

Before I knew it, we were almost on top of Jefferson, and he had opened fire with his fifty-millimeter cannons. I knew he was simultaneously targeting both missiles, which was a fairly routine practice.

Every fifth round was a tracer, and it was a sight to see. You might have sworn he was shooting at *me*, but I knew better. When we were almost in his lap, his cannons had done their job. Both missiles detonated, almost simultaneously, in brief orange explosions.

I zoomed past Jefferson. My ship missed his by the narrowest of margins. My port wing actually passed above his port wing.

He had slanted his Banshee a little to allow that to happen.

My proximity alarm sounded shrilly, but of course I wouldn't have had a chance to change my course, even if I had wanted to.

It was all over in seconds. I experienced an acute sense of relief.

Since my speed was greater than Jefferson's, I soon was much farther from the *Valley Forge* than he was.

Jefferson said, "Back to the *Forge*, Astrid. You did well! We all did."

I cut my engine.

Jefferson rotated his ship again, so that it was pointed in the earlier direction, away from the *Valley Forge*. Then he relit his engines, sped past me, and did a series of amazing maneuvers, some of which I had never before seen executed in a Banshee. Jefferson spun the thing on its axis, like a thrown football, and then he did a barrel roll, which kept him in the same direction, but now at a higher level, and he did a few stunts I had never seen before. And this was all clear to me through my canopy, because his ship was still brightly lit.

Then he said, "Immelmann," and he undertook a beautiful modified Immelmann, which was basically a wingover, and then he said, "I'm on my way back to the ship. See if you can beat me."

I performed a wingover, and I flew back fairly fast, but I wasn't really trying to win any race.

Jefferson was aware of that. He said, "That's all right, Astrid. We can have a real race some other time."

I said, "Sounds great, Captain. You're on."

28

THE FLIGHT BACK

I was profoundly impressed by Jefferson's piloting skills. I had never seen those kinds of abilities demonstrated by anybody in a Banshee, ever. It was almost as though Jefferson was flashing-back to his early days as a pilot. It's not too unusual for younger pilots to engage in foolish stunts—I almost added, "like Jefferson just had done." But as I said, this was beyond the abilities of practically everyone else—and Jefferson was in his mid-fifties.

Nonetheless, I thought the whole display was odd. What captain challenges one of his team members to a race back to the ship, immediately after killing maybe a couple hundred enemy soldiers?

Of course, I had killed the same number, and I wasn't thinking about that at all. No, I was thinking how glad I was that my captain was skilled enough to take out those two remaining missiles. I was thrilled to be alive.

This war continued to be something strange as far as I was concerned, with many curveballs being thrown at me, and little if anything going according to plan. And I noticed a pattern in my behavior. I seemed to want to go beyond what was expected. What's more, in doing so, I was engaging in reckless behavior. I began to wonder whether Jefferson was the crazy one, or me.

I seemed to be fighting this war on my own terms, more than on the Navy's. That was a scary thought, but it was also liberating. I wondered whether I could keep it up —or whether I *should*.

As we flew back toward the *Valley Forge*, I began to wonder whether Jefferson might possibly have regained his sanity. I certainly hoped so. But it was self-delusion. Jefferson's desire to carry out this mission was simply more evidence that he somehow had lost it. I decided to reserve final judgment till we returned.

Jefferson and I maneuvered back into the fighter bay, and all eight Marines were there to welcome us. Lennox and Nash were there as well, and they had already exited their Banshees. There was much joy and shouting.

Captain Jefferson was the last to leave his Banshee.

I was with Waters, reviewing some of the events that had taken place. He said that he and others had monitored everything via feeds from my fighter's cameras.

Captain Jefferson walked directly over to us.

We don't normally salute under such circumstances, but Waters came to attention and saluted Jefferson.

Jefferson returned the salute and said, "As you were, Lieutenant Waters."

Waters said, "Sir, I have rarely—no, never—seen such courage and skill. Congratulations on a successful mission."

Jefferson shook his head and said soberly, "They had

their hands around Amundsen's throat." He produced the Saint Mary medal and said, "I'm returning this. Thanks for the loan."

Waters said, "I hope it helped."

Jefferson smiled slightly and nodded. "I know this much: It didn't hurt."

Waters glanced back at one of the hatches and said, "With your permission, we'll get back to our duties. Talos says eventually more boarding craft will be here."

This appeared to be the moment of truth. Jefferson's reaction to this would perhaps signal his return to normalcy, or a continuation of his downward spiral.

Jefferson said, "Excellent, Lieutenant. Remember, we've narrowly averted a mutiny. The offending parties are still under lock and key, but that leaves the ship with few leaders, and I don't know who I can trust anymore."

Waters said, "Sir, come with us, and you can formulate strategy from the midshipmen's ready-room. Talos says the boarding will be focused on the forward area of the ship. He says the midshipmen's ready-room is the best place for planning."

Jefferson said, "No, no, no, can't do that. A captain's place is on the bridge. I'll be directing our defense from there."

Waters glanced at me. It was apparent that the captain was not to be dissuaded.

"All right, Captain," Waters said. "I'll escort you back to the bridge."

I didn't know what, if anything, Waters was planning, but it didn't matter.

Jefferson said, "Nonsense! What kind of a captain is it that can't find his way back to his own bridge?"

Waters said, "Of course, Captain. That sounds fine."

Jefferson said, "You're both dismissed. Thank you for your support, both of you."

We saluted Jefferson and headed toward the hatch nearest the ready-room, while Captain Jefferson moved toward the forward hatch.

~

I COULDN'T LET it go at that.

I turned from the others and jogged back in the direction Captain Jefferson was headed.

I caught up with him at the hatch, and I said, "Excuse me, Sir?"

Jefferson removed his hand from the hatch and looked at me. He seemed to be smiling slightly, and it looked to me as though he was welcoming the opportunity to speak further.

He said, "Yes, Midshipman Amundsen, what is it?"

I didn't have anything planned that I could say. I just knew that it felt wrong to have Jefferson move out to the bridge, alone. I thought fast, though, and I said, "Sir, we've been lucky so far, as a crew. I suppose every soldier, or in our case, sailor, wants to be with his captain before the battle, during the battle, after the battle. I know we're together here on the *Valley Forge.* But I mean more like Lennox, Nash, and I being guided by you on our attack a little while ago."

"I understand that," Jefferson said, thoughtfully, "but it's time for us to separate."

I was determined not to leave him until he was safely on the bridge. I wasn't sure why. But I knew if I could accompany him there, I could at least observe him a little longer, and perhaps gain some understanding of what was going on with him, and what his plans might be.

I said, "Yes, soon, Captain, but *now*, some words of encouragement from you would be a help, before I attend to my duties."

A great smile appeared on his face, and Jefferson said, "You're a capable fighter, and you have the right spirit. Walk with me to the bridge."

29

IT WAS JUST DOGGEREL

Captain Jefferson and I moved through the corridors. I experienced mixed emotions. I was walking inches from a captain who clearly—from what I could tell—had lost his mind, and whose improvident decisions had cost the lives of two of my friends, as well as eleven other members of the crew. Surely *he* was the one who should have died as a result of his foolhardy actions—and not Adler and Boyle, and the others.

But plainly he was *willing* to die, and he would have been happy to do so by himself in a lone effort to attack the enemy boarding craft. That was bravery. Or maybe it was simply more foolishness or insane behavior. I didn't know.

And if the deaths of my friends were due to insanity, then perhaps it was wrong to blame Jefferson. Moreover, if Jefferson had indeed lost touch with reality, then Commander Rabinowitz should have relieved him of his command.

Of course, if she had done so, then the entire crew would have been branded as cowards, and probably would have been court-martialed. But maybe that would have been preferable to losing the ship and many lives.

These and a hundred other thoughts were plaguing me as we walked toward the bridge.

At last, Jefferson spoke. He said, "The sea is calm tonight. The tide is full. The moon lies fair upon the straits."

As most sailors would, I recognized the words. I said, "Matthew Arnold."

Jefferson said, "Indeed. I learned more from that poem than I did in four years at the Naval Academy and the thirty-five years following."

We walked in silence, through the narrow, quiet corridors, which to me seemed already haunted by the spirits of my comrades who had been killed that day. It dawned on me that this—what I was going through—was simply life. Sometimes you're dealt a bad hand, but you play it as well as you can.

We passed through several hatches, and we closed them behind us. It would have been easy to think that we were alone on the *Valley Forge*—but I knew that, even then, every other man and woman on board were checking and rechecking their shotguns, and wondering whether they would still be alive an hour from now.

The entrance to the bridge lay in front of us, and again quoting or paraphrasing the poet, Jefferson said, "Midshipman Amundsen, the world has no peace, and no help for pain. And we are swept with confused alarms of struggle and flight, where ignorant armies clash by night."

We entered the now-deserted bridge.

I said, "It's a pessimistic poem."

Jefferson said, "Yes. But for warriors, it sums up life. We so often see the darker side of man. Never mind those whose lives began outside of the solar system. If I don't understand mankind, how can I fathom the workings of those from other planetary systems or different galaxies? They've killed so many of us. Yet we've killed many *more* of them." He paused, then added, "And why do we have so few allies on our own planet?"

I said, "That's a question I can't answer."

Jefferson nodded and said, "Now have a seat in the executive officer's chair."

I sat down in the chair that, perhaps two hours earlier, had been occupied by Commander Rabinowitz.

Jefferson stepped to the main viewing port and hit a switch. The port's cover slid out of its position, and we had before us a magnificent view of the starry surroundings.

Jefferson said, "Inspiring, isn't it?"

I said, "Well, outer space has been a muse to many poets."

Jefferson raised his eyebrows. "Do you have a favorite?"

"A favorite poem?" I asked.

"Yes," Jefferson said, "one inspired by the stars."

I said, "I do. It's titled 'Space-Borne.' Do you know it?"

Jefferson nodded and said, "I think I do." He looked upward and said, "Inky blackness, space-borne seas . . . ." He hesitated, trying to call it to mind. "No, I can't recall."

In an effort to prompt him, I said, slowly, "Ten quintillion . . . ."

Jefferson smiled a beautiful smile and said, "Ah, yes, thank you." He said:

"Inky blackness, space-borne seas,

Ten quintillion galaxies,
Sun, and Moon, and lake, and land,
Are all within the Maker's hand.
On Earth, in space, in wide void dim,
I am yet standing next to Him."

I said, "Very nicely recited."

"Do you believe in God, Amundsen?"

I said, "Yes, I do."

Jefferson shook his head slowly. "I don't think I could ever believe in God."

I asked, "You don't? Then why did you cross yourself earlier?"

Jefferson didn't reply to my question. He said, "Why did God put us into this difficulty we're now in?"

I said, "I don't know. I can't explain much of what God does. I don't think I need to. He's God."

Jefferson said, "I know that poem is on a memorial at Annapolis, but whoever wrote it was a fool."

I nodded. "That what my grandmother always says."

Jefferson looked puzzled. "What do you mean by that?"

"My grandfather composed it."

"Oh, apologies, Amundsen," Jefferson said. "I had no idea."

"Oh, that's fine, no offense taken. She always said it was just doggerel."

30

TWELVE LIGHT-YEARS FROM EARTH

Jefferson moved nearer the viewing port. He stared into the distance, silently. Then he turned around and said, "How far are we from your home?"

"My home?"

"Yes, where are you from? Where do you want to return to? Of course, wherever it is on Earth, we're about the same distance from it. But I'm curious."

I said, "I was born in Santa Monica."

"California. A beautiful state. How far are we from there?"

I said, "Close to twelve light-years at the moment."

Jefferson again turned his back at an angle to me and stared into the vastness of space. "That distance can't really be comprehended, can it?"

"No," I said, "it can't."

Talos came onto 1MC (the ship-wide channel) and said, "Five enemy boarding ships and twenty enemy fighters, eighteen minutes out at current speed."

We were nearing the culmination of the day's activities. For good or ill, it would all be over soon. This was not the way I had ever pictured my final moments alive—discussing trivial matters with a crazed captain.

I said, "Time is short, Captain, so with your permission I'll rejoin the others."

Jefferson shook his head. "Eighteen minutes are a lifetime. The fighters are only there to protect the boarding ships. They aren't a real threat. They won't launch missiles at the *Valley Forge*, because at this point they want to avoid damaging our ship any more than necessary. They want to take the ship whole, and along with it an FTL drive that we don't even possess. Remember what Arnold said: *Ignorant armies clash by night.*"

At that, Jefferson laughed softly. I think he saw that the human race hadn't really learned anything since Arnold's time.

"And after the boarding ships attach," Jefferson said, "it will take them at least five minutes to penetrate the hull. And that's if everything goes smoothly. And nothing ever does."

I said, "True enough."

Jefferson grew thoughtful. He said, "I wonder why they chose this particular location for this training mission. Why twelve light-years from Earth? If the Academy wants to train its midshipmen, why couldn't they do that a half-million miles from Earth, instead? The experience is the same. Space is the same here and near the planet Earth, right?"

Now Jefferson was beginning to talk my language. Why twelve light-years, indeed?

And the way Jefferson expressed it, it seemed that there was only one explanation—the very reason that I had been toying with. Specifically, we were pawns in a broader Navy program. It all fit. The *Valley Forge* was an obsolescent ship. We had no faster-than-light capability. We had been supplied with a mere sixteen Banshees, several of which didn't function. We were twelve light-years from our planet, and there was no evident reason for that.

Something didn't fit. Something was wrong.

Was Captain Jefferson's weird behavior a component in a broader Navy scheme? If so, that would imply that something had been done, by *someone*, to bring about this mental state in the captain.

Was this man even Captain Jefferson in the first place? Maybe he was Jefferson's insane twin. Or maybe he was an android or a cyborg, or perhaps an evil clone. Had someone done away with the real Captain Jefferson? As weird as these ideas were, they actually seemed plausible to me.

If my premise was that his strange mental state did not represent the authentic mental state of Captain Jefferson, then what could be its cause? The ones I had outlined in my mind seemed far-fetched, if not flatly incredible.

And then I came up with solutions that seemed more likely. Pharmaceuticals. An alien infection. Who knows what the real explanation might be? But whether I was right, or whether I was completely wrong, it seemed *possible* that it was something like that.

I didn't have any reasonable way of validating these theories. I couldn't say to Jefferson, *Uh, Captain, you've been acting insane lately. Would you mind submitting to a blood test to see whether some alien organism has attacked you?*

Besides, at that moment I wasn't at all sure what would be achieved by that.

Jefferson said, "Did you hear me?"

I said, "I apologize, Captain Jefferson. Yes, indeed, I did hear you. But your question started my brain on a whole sequence of thoughts, puzzling thoughts. In response to your statement, yes, space is the same here, twelve light-years away, as it is, say, two or three light-seconds from Earth—at least, it's the same for our purposes. We could be the same distance from Earth that the Moon is, and experience the same training. Perhaps better training, dealing with more-complex orbital mechanics."

"Precisely," Jefferson said. "And if we were near the Moon or even Mars, we could at least serve in a support role for our ships that are assigned to Moon or Mars protection. We're just one small ship, but, you know, sometimes one man with a paddle, in a little coracle, can save the day."

"Right," I said. "For want of a nail, a kingdom was lost, as they say. Just one little horseshoe nail could have turned defeat into victory."

Jefferson nodded and said, contemplatively, "One little horseshoe nail."

31

MOMENTARY LUCIDITY

Even though Jefferson seemed to be jumping from subject to subject, there was a lucidity about him, and about the things he was saying, that told me he was different now, at least for the moment.

Jefferson sat down in the captain's chair. He began rapping his fingers on the arm of the chair. Then he patted his head and said to me, "I don't think decompression is a worry yet. Maybe in a little while." He gestured toward me and said, "Get your helmet on as soon as you're back with the others."

I nodded. "Will do, Captain." At this point I was glad that I had stayed with Jefferson. Even though he was still acting rather weird, I figured that sometime I would look into my suspicions that someone evil was behind Jefferson's departure from his former self.

Jefferson said, "Without your helmet, you look awfully young."

I said, "I'm nearly twenty-one."

"Still," Jefferson said, "too young to go out and die."

I shrugged. "What must be, must be, I suppose."

Jefferson said, "But I picture you, some years from now, commanding your own warship, one like the *Valley Forge*, perhaps, or even bigger."

"Sounds good, but I expect to enter the Marines on graduation."

Jefferson smiled and said, "How can the Navy survive, if the Marines keep siphoning off our best people?"

I said, "I'm flattered."

"Nonsense," Jefferson said. "Can't you see that you're different from the others?"

"Different?" I asked.

Jefferson coughed out a dismissive laugh. "You don't see it. The truly gifted ones never do. They're full of self-criticism. They see too much good in others. They're too self-sacrificial. And by the way, if you don't watch out with all your volunteering, you're not going to survive—stay alive—more than two or three years. Life isn't as good as you think it is." He paused, then added, "And I suppose it's not as *bad* as *I* think it is."

I now felt I had done my bit. Jefferson was all squared away. And I had received more than my daily allotment of undeserved adulation, with a little counseling thrown in.

Almost as though he had read my mind, Jefferson said, "I think it's time for me to get back to my monitors. You know, I'm handling everything by myself, now that the other bridge officers are confined. There are a few other officers on board who are still loyal to their captain—you and Lennox and Nash, among them, and Waters and his people—but they now have specific duties that they need to attend to. But I think I'm up to the challenges of the bridge."

I said, "All right, then. Sounds good. I'd better—"

Jefferson interrupted, asking, "What's your favorite novel?"

I thought, *Great, now what?* I said, "I don't know. Maybe *A Tale of Two Cities*. I'm reading that now."

Jefferson said, "Ah, yes. Sydney Carton. 'A far, far better rest that I go to.' My own favorite is *Don Quixote*. That book contains everything you need to know about how to be a great captain. Of course, Quixote was insane, but that's part of the magic of that book."

Quixote was indeed insane, though it appeared to me that Jefferson's comment was the pot calling the kettle black.

Jefferson continued, saying, "Quixote's main problem was in thinking that the windmills were giants. You see, he couldn't tell who his real enemies were."

I said, "I suppose not." But I wasn't sure exactly how much discernment Jefferson himself had, since he had mistaken the Kerleegan warships for creampuffs.

"That's what you need to do as a commander," Jefferson said. "Know who your friends are, and who your enemies are."

I said, "Good advice, Captain."

Jefferson nodded and said, "I expect it's time for you to rejoin your people. I'll need to stay here on the bridge. That's where the captain belongs. Agreed?"

I said, "Agreed, Sir."

Jefferson held up his palm, indicating that I should wait. "Before you go," he said, "one more thing. Come with me to my berth. I want you to have something."

~

Captain Jefferson's berth was near the bridge. He also had a more formal cabin, somewhat larger, fifty yards aft. What we called his berth was actually a small office, with a narrow bed, and with a lot of electronics. If necessary, Jefferson could run an entire campaign without leaving this compartment. He could control weapons, navigation—everything.

Jefferson had me wait by the hatch while he stepped inside. He pulled open a desk drawer, and reverently removed from it an American flag, folded into the familiar triangle of the tricorn hat worn by the Patriots. All that was visible were white stars and the blue field.

When he returned to the hatchway, Jefferson handed the flag to me, saying, "This is the flag that was placed over my son's casket when his remains were returned home."

I asked, "Returned home? What happened?"

"This was during the first attack by the Kerleegans on a United States vessel."

"The *Adirondack*?"

"Yes," Jefferson said. "She was a lone ship, like the *Valley Forge*. There were eleven Kerleegan ships. Six carriers. Five cruisers."

For a moment, that struck me as highly strange. That was the same configuration as the Kerleegan task force that engaged us. Then it dawned on me that this may have been the cause of Jefferson's strange behavior. On some level, he wanted the *Valley Forge* to avenge his son's death.

I asked, "What was your son's name?"

"My wife and I named him Quentin. That was a bad choice. It stemmed from egotism on my part. And my wife couldn't call me by name without mentioning her dead son's name at the same time. It was bad. But that was then."

I said, "Captain Jefferson, I'm so sorry. I didn't know any of this."

Jefferson nodded. "Few do. And those who knew at one time have now forgotten. Not me, of course. Not my poor wife." He laughed softly. "Just as we said, Amundsen—one little horseshoe-nail. That's us. That's the *Valley Forge*. We need to win this battle. We don't want anyone to say, ever, 'if only the *Valley Forge* had been here.' And they won't say that, if I have anything to do with it. And to make certain that we're there at that future battle, when we're needed, we will prevail today. We need to plant Old Glory in the hallowed ground that is the *Valley Forge*. We need to close ranks around the ensign, and protect the *Forge*, whatever may come."

Carrying the flag, I retraced my steps and arrived back at the fighter bay. I cut through the bay, and soon I was back in the midshipmen's ready-room.

My mind was alive with thoughts on the complexities of human behavior, and the things that contribute to the waging of battles, and the motivations of those who participate in them.

32

CAPTAIN JEFFERSON AND ADMIRAL FARRAGUT

All eight Marines, as well as Lennox and Nash, were in the ready-room when I entered. In my right hand was my M90, and with my left arm I was holding Jefferson's flag against my stomach.

Lennox gestured toward the flag and asked, "What's that about?"

I set the flag down on the table, and I briefly summarized what Captain Jefferson had told me regarding his son and the flag.

Lennox said, "Good to have Old Glory to rally around."

Several of the others made similar comments.

I said, "We can keep her here while we work out our collective future." The midshipmen's ready-room had become our headquarters.

Waters said, "In spite of the success out there with Captain Jefferson in destroying those boarding ships, we can assume that boarding the *Valley Forge* will be the enemy's next step. I noticed that a lot of the shotguns are gone from the racks. Plenty are still there, but obviously the rest of the crew is ready to repel boarders."

I said, "Okay, so far, so good."

Waters said, "Talos, what's our position with regard to defense systems?"

Talos said, "All sixty of our defensive drones have been destroyed. We still have six observation drones. All of our missile countermeasures are exhausted."

Waters said, "So, we have a no-go on the drones. What about missiles?"

"We have none."

"Talos," I said, "let me try to summarize our situation, and then you'll tell me whether my summary is accurate."

Talos said, "Proceed."

I said, "Boiled down, we have five turrets and six observation drones. And we have a dozen or so operable Banshees, with cannons but with no missiles. Is that about right?"

"Yes, Ma'am," Talos said, "and also many small arms and other weapons—M90s, shotguns, grenades, and so on. From this point on, whatever else you do, make them pay an extortionate price."

That didn't sound promising. We started with hundreds of missiles, and we remained behind the eight ball. Now all we had available was modern warfare's version of squirt guns and peashooters. What could we accomplish with those?

"Got that," I said. "Tell me, Talos, how are we doing?"

Talos said, "Putting it in simple terms, we have destroyed more of the enemy's assets than they have destroyed of ours. But they had far more assets to lose. The initial odds against us were forty-eight to one. Now the odds stand at about a hundred-and-thirty to one."

I said, "Initially, I was figuring twenty-nine to one. Now you're saying it was originally forty-eight to one."

Talos said, "The rule of thumb you were applying was something the Navy likes to promote. Makes the enemy seem weaker than they are. Better for morale. But mark my words. If you confine the fighting to the interior of this ship, and if you kill a great many of their soldiers, and continue to do so, at some point they will depart."

"We better choose the areas that are the most defendable," I said.

Waters said, "Talos, you can keep us informed on which sections of the ship have an enemy presence, right?"

"Yes, Lieutenant Waters."

Even though there were eleven of us in the ready-room, few were saying anything. Occasionally someone would make a brief remark or ask a simple question. The replies were terse. Then even those brief exchanges stopped, and all was quiet.

The ready-room had chairs against the bulkheads and at the table. Most of us were seated in those chairs, though at any given moment there were one or two people standing.

The whole situation reminded me of my second year at the Academy. I was a member of the Masqueraders, which is the Academy's extracurricular theater group. I was in a room with about six others, and we were waiting for our auditions for a play called *Atlantic Shore*. I was nervous.

Even though the other auditioning midshipmen and I knew each other well, few people said anything, and there were no real conversations. We were all focused on our "sides," which are basically extracts from the script—and on being, in theater terms, "comfortable, confident, and charismatic." We had that edginess, that tenseness that is uncomfortable, but which leads to better results.

Waters broke the silence. He asked, "Talos, is Captain Jefferson still on the bridge?"

"Yes," Talos said, "he is alone there."

"What's he doing?"

"He appears to be engaged in a conversation with a portrait of Admiral Farragut."

I said, "That doesn't sound good."

"No, Ma'am," Talos said, "it doesn't."

Waters said, "I have to go get him. And we're gonna need to consolidate our forces in the stern. Then we can decompress the rest of the ship if we decide to, and not have to worry about rapid decompression. All right, guys, stay afloat."

I said to Waters, "You're taking me with you."

Nash said, "Me, too."

Waters smiled at Nash and said, "Nash, you're like Amundsen. Well, not quite. In fact, nowhere near. But still, you're all right. Let's go."

33

BACK TO THE BRIDGE

The three of us moved out. My mind was racing. Each time we came to a hatch, I wondered whether there were enemy soldiers on the other side. Talos kept telling us there weren't, but I didn't believe him entirely.

I was holding my M90 automatic-rifle. It's a small and light weapon, and that's why I decided to take it to the bridge. A shotgun would provide more stopping-power, but those are more cumbersome. Also, when fully loaded, the shotguns are two or three times as heavy.

We continued from corridor to compartment to corridor, and we made our way to the bridge.

I didn't know what to expect there.

A captain who orders his lone ship into action against eleven enemy ships is unusual, to say the least. But there's nothing unlawful about it—probably.

But a captain who is conversing with a portrait of Admiral Farragut? In the middle of a pitched battle? Draw your own conclusions, but I'd say it's likely that this was conclusive proof that the man had taken leave of his sanity and was unfit to lead. I braced myself for the likelihood that Captain Jefferson would issue a series of insane orders.

Waters and I entered the bridge, while Nash kept watch at the entrance. Except for Jefferson, the bridge was deserted. It was strange to see the empty chairs, especially those of the captain and the other bridge officers. Even then, the other officers might still be in the brig—though not locked in—if they had not already departed there to repel boarders.

I looked quickly from chair to chair. They definitely gave the place a deserted atmosphere, leaving one with the question, "Who is piloting this thing?" And the answer to that question was, "Nobody."

Not that it mattered. Even though the *Valley Forge* was moving at a high velocity relative to the nearest celestial bodies—which were distant, by the way—there was nothing near enough to show us that we were moving at all. We didn't really need a pilot or navigator. We weren't close to anything except the enemy.

On one of the rear bulkheads of the bridge were small framed portraits of American naval leaders, namely Captain John Paul Jones, Captain James Lawrence, and Admiral David G. Farragut. Jefferson was standing in front of the portrait of Farragut—who was well known for issuing the order, "Damn the torpedoes, full speed ahead!" This was during the Battle of Mobile Bay. Those probably weren't Farragut's precise words, but those represent the most dramatic version.

So there was Captain Jefferson, conferring with Farragut. Jefferson was saying things like, "I issued your orders, Admiral, but my men refused to carry them out. We would have routed the enemy if my people had simply carried out their orders. If only *you* were here,

Admiral. The men would respect *you*." Jefferson seemed completely unaware that we were present, and he was repeating himself.

Waters and I watched this display for about a minute, unsure of how to proceed. Then Jefferson looked over at Waters. Jefferson seemed to recognize him, and he addressed Waters, saying, "Admiral, you've come, in my hour of need. God bless you, my loyal friend. You'll see, we're in a bit of a fix. But you'll know what to do."

I was stunned to realize that Captain Jefferson believed that Lieutenant Waters was Admiral Farragut.

Then Captain Jefferson stared silently at Waters, who unsurprisingly said nothing.

Then Jefferson summarized our position, saying, rather clearly, I thought, given the circumstances, "We've been attacked by a force much more numerous than ours, eleven ships to our one. Six are carriers. In strength the enemy force is over one hundred times ours at this point in the battle. We've lost all four ventral turrets, all four dorsal turrets, two starboard turrets, and one port turret."

Waters looked at me briefly, bewildered.

Nash turned around from his position at the entrance to the bridge and stared at me momentarily.

I just stood there, trying to look as military as possible, glad that Jefferson was addressing Waters, and not me.

Jefferson continued, saying, "We've expended all of our missiles, as well as all of our missile countermeasures. Our point-defense drones all have been destroyed. We've managed to destroy twelve of the enemy's boarding craft. But now we're about to be boarded. Combat will be hand to hand. I have done my best, but I have failed. In this, my darkest hour, I ask for your help. Admiral, I'm turning command of the *Valley Forge* over to you."

I have to hand it to Waters. He stepped into the breach and *became* Admiral Farragut.

Waters said, sternly, "No, Captain Jefferson, you have *not* failed. Never believe anything different. A few of your men failed *you*. That is all. At your request, I am assuming command of the *Valley Forge*. I and my subordinates here will escort you to a place where you can rest—where you can sleep. We will wake you when the battle is over. Already I have reports that the tide is turning, due to your leadership. Are you ready to go now?"

Jefferson said, "I am, Admiral. I am indeed. Thank you for your words of encouragement. I will *never* forget them."

34

REMORSE AND SHAME

Honestly, I am not an emotional person when it comes to military matters, but I found this entire scene—Nash at the entry, and Waters and me, faced by Captain Jefferson—the most heartbreaking situation I had ever witnessed. There I was with my M90, with enemy soldiers at that moment probably affixing their boarding craft to the *Valley Forge*, and with Nash likely jumpier than a grasshopper—and yet I was barely able to keep from weeping at the exchange between Waters and the captain whom I had been wasting my energy hating and accusing.

I was ashamed of myself for the things I had been thinking about our unfortunate captain, whom I and the rest of the bridge staff had made no effort to understand, and whom we were ready to desert an hour or two earlier.

Then Captain Jefferson looked at me, and I was petrified regarding what he might say or think.

Jefferson looked back at Waters and said, "But I see you have had help. This is Midshipman Amundsen. Do you know her? She was one of my pupils. She was my brightest student." He paused and stared upward wistfully, as though he were reliving some pleasant happening. Then he said, "I always was proud of her. Of my entire crew, she is the very best. She *alone* supported me on the bridge, and moved bravely to prepare the other midshipmen for the fight. And then, listen to me, Amundsen led an attack on enemy boarding craft, in which four enemy vessels were destroyed. I saw and heard it all on my monitors. And after that, she and I led a raid in which eight Kerleegan boarding ships were destroyed. We returned with no casualties on our side." His voice grew soft, and faded almost to silence. Then, a little louder, he said, slowly and clearly, "I'll be recommending her for the Navy Cross."

And in light of that, in spite of all my will to the contrary, tears actually came to my eyes, and I was definitely weeping. I summoned all my strength to stifle it, and I tried not to show what I was going through, but I'm sure I didn't fool Waters.

I couldn't help myself. Such undeserved praise was torture. Then I swallowed hard and cleared my throat, resolving to move ahead and put my remorse and shame behind me.

We all said nothing.

Then Waters said, "I'm sure Midshipman Amundsen has earned that medal. We'll discuss that later. Now we need to go to a place where you can rest."

And the four of us moved out. As we proceeded through the ship, I wondered whether I might have been better off, had I not gone with Waters to retrieve Captain Jefferson.

~

We took Jefferson to the berth that Lennox and I had been sharing, and we made him comfortable. At my suggestion, Waters contacted Gray and Guzman, who had seemed like compassionate men when I found them taking care of Boyle. They met us there with sedatives.

I pulled Guzman into the corridor. I briefly explained my concern that someone might have inflicted this mental condition on Captain Jefferson, and that it might not be simply an abnormality that originated with Jefferson.

Guzman was highly interested, and he asked me various questions about Captain Jefferson's behavior. I answered those questions as well as I could.

When Waters, Nash, and I left them, Captain Jefferson was sleeping peacefully.

35

CLOAKED AND UNDETECTABLE

From the berth in which we left Captain Jefferson, it was only a few steps to the midshipmen's ready-room. We entered without ceremony and found the rest of the Marines, as well as Lennox. All were studying a monitor that showed an outline of the *Valley Forge*, and which indicated, according to Talos's analysis, the most likely places of entry for enemy boarding parties.

Since the engines and reactors were near the stern, that was an unlikely area for entry. Those facilities were far more heavily armored than most of the ship. Certain other areas—such as launch platforms—were also well armored. These were common-sense places for additional armor, and the Kerleegans didn't need any spies to give them that information. The image on the screen demonstrated that all of the likely points of entry were forward of the fighter bays.

Talos said, "Attention, all crew. Five Kerleegan boarding craft are now eight minutes out. They are accompanied by twenty fighter craft."

Lennox said, "Twenty fighters. Not very many."

I said, "They know we only have five turrets left."

Then Commander Rabinowitz stepped into the ready-room, and behind her were Commanders Silver and Newton.

I called out, "Officers on deck, attention to orders!"

All came to attention and saluted. The new arrivals returned the salutes.

None of the Marines and none of the midshipmen said anything further. My own reason for saying nothing additional was that the situation was so unusual. I flat-out didn't know what to say. Something like, *Congratulations, you escaped the brig* occurred to me, but it didn't seem right.

We all remained at attention, though, until Rabinowitz said, "As you were."

At that point, Waters, who had made certain their cells had remained unlocked, said, "Glad to have you here, Ma'am."

Rabinowitz said, "What's Captain Jefferson's status?"

Waters summarized the situation.

Rabinowitz said, "That simplifies things. With the captain on the tranquilizers, I'm simply filling in for him while he is indisposed, or absent. No formalities needed."

Waters said, "Yes, Ma'am."

Rabinowitz took a seat at the table and said, "Anyone who wants to sit, feel free."

Newton and Silver sat. So did Lennox, Nash, and I. A few of the Marines sat, and a few remained standing.

I took that opportunity to tell the new arrivals about the flag. They all approved.

I said, "Talos, tell me something."

"Just ask."

"You've said that the Kerleegans are in a 'boarding mode' now, right?"

"Yes," Talos said, "and that is based on the makeup of this task force, their tactics so far in this battle, and their tactics overall in this war."

I drummed my fingers against the tabletop. "And they'll keep trying to board us until they defeat us, or until they decide that their losses are too great?"

"Correct," Talos said.

I asked, "Then how do we bring about that second situation? Is it based on damage to their equipment, loss of personnel, loss of leaders—what?"

"We don't have much data on this," Talos said. "But the pattern I see is that they depart when they experience massive personnel losses. And that's about as detailed as I can make it."

I asked, "Talos, you have some kind of built-in strategy for implementing decompression, right?"

"Well," Talos said, "not specifically for decompression. I figure it out on the fly, to the best of my capabilities."

I asked, "Which sections of the ship can be decompressed suddenly and violently? The fighter bays, I assume, but any others?"

Talos said, "The fighter bays are the principal areas that fit that description. Any hatch that we open will quickly decompress connected compartments. But since most of the exterior hatches connect to airlocks, the process is not a simple one, if you want to decompress a large area."

Rabinowitz said, "What would the process be for decompressing the fighter bays?"

"We open the outer doors," Talos said, "and leave the

forcefields in place to maintain pressure. We seal the hatches leading into the bays. Then at the right time, we disable the forcefields."

An idea was rattling around in my brain, but it would not crystalize. I asked, "Which compartments and corridors have wall-mounted pressure-gauges?"

Talos said, "All have at least one pressure-gauge. Almost all airlocks have three or more, one for pressure inside the airlock, and one to show the pressure of each adjoining compartment or corridor."

Everyone was quiet. It was as though we saw some kind of a useful tactic buried in that information, but couldn't quite put our finger on it.

But a plan began to form in my head. I said, "What if we leave all of the airlocks operational? If they scan for life forms, they'll see that no one is in the front two-thirds of the ship. Then they'll want to use the airlocks to move into one or both of the fighter bays, if they want to gain control of the engines and reactors. We seal off the bays, then decompress them—violently."

Waters shook his head and said, "There are a lot of uncertainties. I don't like it. But I guess we have nothing to lose."

Talos said, over 1MC, "Attention, all crew. Four Kerleegan boarding craft and twenty fighter craft are now five minutes out."

I said, "Four boarding craft? What happened to the fifth one?"

Talos said, "It is cloaked and undetectable."

36

THE GRATIFYING EXPLOSION

Then, over 1MC, Rabinowitz said, "This is Commander Rabinowitz. All crew who are now forward of the fighter bays are ordered to move to positions aft of the bays. All likely points of enemy boarding are forward of the fighter bays. I'll see you all after the fight."

I said, "Let's see. After the gunners vacate the forward turrets, only the two port-turrets will be manned."

Rabinowitz said, "Are you suggesting something?"

I said, "I don't know, Ma'am. Does Talos have protocols for ship rotation to take full advantage of the two remaining port guns? Or we could bring all five remaining side-turrets to bear, if we maneuver the *Valley Forge* so that either the dorsal face or the ventral face is turned toward the enemy. Talos could operate the unoccupied turrets remotely."

Rabinowitz said, "Talos? If you can accomplish that, do so."

Talos said, "I don't have programming that deals with

this scenario, but I'll do the necessary calculations." After a brief pause, Talos said, "Calculations complete. I've instructed the two remaining turret-gunners to vacate their turrets, and to stand by to help with reloading. I will operate all five guns. That will ensure that all turrets will be working cooperatively. I am maneuvering the ship to create the smallest possible theoretical silhouette consistent with bringing all five guns to bear. I will continue to use the reaction-control thrusters to maintain the most favorable position throughout the attack."

Rabinowitz said, "Very good."

Waters said, "Yes, that'll provide the maximum protection against whatever comes at us. If they want to amass a large number of troops at any time during this operation, the logical places are the bays. If they do that, then Talos blows the forcefields, and they lose a lot of troops. If they want to trickle the people through little by little, we eliminate them a few at a time—with our shotguns, hopefully from behind the barricades."

Waters looked over at me. I think he wanted to gauge my reaction.

I smiled weakly. Moments earlier, Waters had expressed misgivings regarding my idea of decompressing the bays. Then he gave the concept a coat of paint and stated it in different words, and all of a sudden he's Copernicus.

Then Rabinowitz spoke up. "Lieutenant Waters, help me out. How is that different from what Midshipman Amundsen suggested?"

"I guess it's not," Waters said with a sheepish smile.

I was about to say something in Waters's defense, because I hated to see him put on the spot. But before I could open my mouth, the sounds of battle began again.

The main noise at first was the horrendous racket of the *Valley Forge*'s guns. The guns were behemoths with multiple barrels, and with an aggregate rate of fire of ninety rounds per second, per gun.

Since there were no flares, and indeed no lights of any kind, our viewing was limited to the representations of the output of the sensors, as displayed on our monitors. There wasn't much that could be made out. Again, it was like watching bees swarming.

But we could see the boarding craft as they maneuvered insidiously to make contact with the ventral area, which was the optimum side for their activities.

Inwardly I was slightly amused at the difficulty they were having in attaching themselves. Talos's constant partial rotations of the *Valley Forge* gave them a difficult time.

Using the RCS thrusters, Talos could rapidly change the orientation of the *Valley Forge*, and more than once this resulted in our ship actually "batting" the boarding craft while they maneuvered for position. We could see this represented on the screens, and whenever the contact was made, there was a terrible crashing sound. The noise was such that you would have thought that the *Valley Forge* was being ripped open, but it was nothing to the *Forge*, which was built to absorb massive impacts.

Not so, the boarding craft, however. There, the contacts were colossal and potentially back-breaking.

Talos didn't narrate any of this, but I think he knew well that this was turning out to be effective.

Of course, on board we didn't even notice the changes in the ship's orientation, other than on the monitors. The artificial gravity within the *Valley Forge* always pulled us toward the deck, and the inertia dampeners covered most of the other effects.

The damaging force of Talos's blows became more evident when one of the boarding ships, having suffered a particularly brutal clubbing, drifted away from the *Valley Forge* in a straight trajectory, and in a tumbling fashion.

Waters remotely adjusted the one of the cameras to isolate that particular craft. I think all of us were transfixed by the strangeness of what had happened.

I was staring at the monitor from four feet away, and I sucked in my breath in surprise when that boarding ship exploded in an enormous detonation of—I assume—its fuel supply. I imagined the terror of the boarders as the propellent and oxygen tanks ruptured, and their contents made contact with the ship's rocket-blast.

It was highly gratifying.

"Commander Rabinowitz," Talos said, "the Kerleegan fighters are now beyond the effective range of the guns. Moreover, I am no longer able to acquire any boarding craft as targets for the guns, because of their location."

Rabinowitz said, "Can you make any other recommendations?"

Talos said, "Ma'am, allow me to offer a tactics alternative. You may wish to light the engines. I can then impart a spin to the *Valley Forge*. I can, in fact, bring about a rapid rotation, so that we will move through space, spinning, like a bullet does. Under those conditions it will be impossible for the boarding craft to attach themselves."

That suggestion had a nice flavor to it, but it would never work. It basically relied on the Kerleegans to give up and go away. So, when I heard that I didn't like it. Then the only course of action available to the Kerleegans would be to pursue us.

There were plenty of Kerleegan fighters still in the vicinity. With our engines lit, the nozzles wouldn't be shielded. Right now we not only had the forcefield shielding the engines, but temporary armor plates were in place over the nozzles to offer further protection. In short, if we tried what Talos was suggesting, we were goners. There were no two ways about that.

Rabinowitz said, "Talos, is that what you're recommending?"

"No, Ma'am," Talos said. "It's just an idea. There is a downside, as long as the Kerleegan task force is in the vicinity."

Rabinowitz said, "That's what I thought. I'm rejecting that suggestion."

Then an announcement came over 1MC. It was Talos's voice again. "Attention all crew, enemy boarding craft are attaching. Prepare to repel boarders."

37

DEFENDING SECTION 'N'

I suppose it had been inevitable that sooner or later the Kerleegan ships would manage to attach. After the first one attached, the remaining other two of the original four managed to do so as well, in short order.

We soon heard the enemy drilling, as the sounds were carried through the hull. It was hard to tell precisely where the sounds were coming from, but images on our monitors pinpointed the activity. The attached ships were not relying on stealth technology at this point.

There were three boarding craft accounted for, all on the ventral surface of the *Valley Forge*. The sounds were horrible beyond imagination. They were howls, screeches, roars. And I heard repeated booms as though colossal hammers were hitting the hull.

I said, "Talos, where is the *fifth* boarding craft? And is there still a fighter escort? Our monitors here show nothing."

Talos said, "The fifth craft is cloaked. The fighter escort is staying far back. The fact that they are keeping their distance tends to confirm my view that if you can destroy all, or nearly all, enemy personnel from all five boarding craft, the Kerleegans will depart."

Commander Rabinowitz said, "Keep us informed."

Talos said, "Aye aye, Ma'am."

The Kerleegans had several different types of tools for penetrating enemy hulls. Ordinarily they would change drill bits, depending on the makeup of each layer of the hull, and they also used drilling torches, which generated great heat. Penetrating a hull was a time-consuming process, and it could take five or ten minutes, or more, to establish an opening. It was a nightmarish position for us to be in, waiting for the hair-raising sounds to stop, and knowing that when they did, it simply meant that the ship was going to be taking on scores of enemy troops.

There were now fourteen of us in the midshipmen's ready-room—the eight Marines, the three commanders from the bridge, and the three midshipmen, including me. Our current inability to do something, to take action of some kind, was frustrating and maddening.

I said to Waters, "What about taking out the Banshees again?"

Waters said, "I've been thinking about that myself. But there isn't any circumstance I can imagine that would allow us to do that. We fooled them once, but they wouldn't let us get away with that again." Then Waters looked upward and said, "Talos, your thoughts?"

"Lieutenant Waters, my analysis is the same as yours," Talos said. "Although several Banshees are available, none have missiles mounted. They do have their guns, but then so do the boarding craft. Also, the Kerleegan fighters are still out there, and we do not want to draw them back in."

Waters said, "Okay," and I gave up on that plan. For several seconds, no one said anything.

Then Talos said, "Enemy boarding ship attempting hull penetration in section N."

That was in our stern area, which we had thought was safe from boarding attempts.

I said, "I guess we now know where the fifth boarding ship is."

Commander Rabinowitz said, "Midshipman Amundsen, take your people and go back to section N, please. Make them regret trying to penetrate our hull there." The she turned to Lieutenant Waters. "Lieutenant Waters, how do you view the role of the Marines at this time?"

"For the sake of a unified approach, the Marines will cooperate with you in every way."

Rabinowitz said, "Excellent. I won't give you orders. I'll make recommendations."

Waters said, "Go ahead and give orders, Ma'am. The Marines will carry them out."

Rabinowitz nodded. "For now, I want the Marines to accompany Midshipman Amundsen and her people to section N."

Waters said, "Thank you. That gives me exactly what I wanted."

38

THE UNOFFICIAL LEADER

For the first time, I accepted the fact that I had become the leader of the midshipmen. There was nothing official about it. We were all precisely the same rank. It all started when Captain Jefferson called me to the bridge earlier, at the beginning of this ordeal. From there on, I was pushy and bossy, an officious intermeddler. I tried to deny that I was the leader, but now that was difficult.

The ready-room was not in immediate danger of decompression, and a few of us had not been wearing our helmets. But as soon as the attack on section N was announced, we began to remedy that situation. Most of us already had our shotguns in our hands. Those who didn't, grabbed theirs. By the time Rabinowitz issued her orders, we were all set.

Waters and I, and our people, moved toward section N with a sense of high urgency.

The fictitious phantasm that haunted my thoughts now was a supernatural drill-bit that could cut through our hull like a red-hot poker thrust into cottage cheese.

And I pictured the enemy soldiers, like a swarm of hornets, pouring through the opening.

The reality was different, more predictable, more real.

In accord with normal procedures, the *Valley Forge* crew had decompressed section N, in preparation for the fight against the anticipated boarders. Even though all members of the crew were wearing EVA suits, rapid decompression could be disastrous for those in the compartment. All this being the case, the Marines and midshipmen had to enter through an airlock.

When we arrived inside, we found four crewmen, each armed with a shotgun. Several more shotguns, about ten, were leaning against bulkheads and machinery.

The crewmen had cleared an area of about ten feet in all directions from the projected point of penetration. There wasn't any doubt as to precisely where the entry was to be.

I walked to the center of the cleared area, and from that place, the racket was ear shattering, even though there was no air to aid in sound transmission. I could feel the vibrations of the deck, which were more like a violent rattling of the surface. A continuous high-pitched whine provided background noise for the sounds of the drill bit, and I could see the deck bowing slightly inward and vibrating. The shields and armor had been penetrated, and all that was left was a bit of open space, and the deck.

I stepped back, since I realized that their drill bit soon would be punching through. I moved to a place near Lennox. We looked briefly at each other, then turned back to watching the cleared area.

Then, with a bang, the huge drill-bit punched through and thrust upward about four feet into the compartment. Then it withdrew completely.

Standard procedure called for us all to conceal ourselves, since the next thing to make its appearance was likely to be a periscope or a camera. Our training was to allow as many boarders to enter as possible, and when we were spotted, to open fire. Accordingly, we all hid as well as we could, and the last words anyone said were from Waters.

He said, "Wait for my command to fire."

39

A FINE JIG BETWEEN HEAVEN AND HELL

Sure enough, up came a slender gooseneck with a camera lens at the end. It snaked upward about a foot, then panned in a full circle, then withdrew.

Next came a soldier. His helmet-covered head emerged, and he peered around carefully. Then, having decided it was safe, he climbed completely into the compartment, then looked back into the boarding ship and said something. Then a weapon, possibly a plasma gun of some kind, was handed up to the first soldier. This process was repeated, and soon there were three enemy soldiers in the compartment. They accomplished all this with great swiftness.

The first three started to search the compartment, and at the same time a fourth enemy soldier began to emerge. I knew that within a second or two we would be found out.

Waters yelled, "Fire!"

Before the word was fully formed, the fifteen of us had discharged our weapons, and most, if not all, of those initial rounds made contact with a Kerleegan helmet.

Our attack was merciless, brutal, savage. The noise was subdued, since the surrounding vacuum did nothing for the transmission of the sound. But the muzzle flash from the barrels of fifteen shotguns lit up the compartment in a most macabre way.

We continued our assault. Each of us adopted whatever shooting position we preferred, and we launched a flood of slugs and buckshot at the three, and also at the fourth Kerleegan, who had attempted, unsuccessfully, to pull himself back into the boarding ship.

Our terrible fusillade drew to a close. All of our side emerged from our places of concealment.

The original three enemy soldiers were dead, or at least were knocked over and weren't moving. A couple of us put additional shotgun blasts into vulnerable places on the enemy suits.

Waters moved to the opening in the deck, where the fourth Kerleegan, in the words of an old song, "danced a fine jig between heaven and hell."

Then Waters did something I'm unlikely to forget. He bent over and grabbed the fourth guy by his arms and yanked him violently up through the opening. In a continuing motion, Waters slammed him down onto the deck. There the invader lay on his stomach, weaponless, with Waters standing above him.

I didn't see him grab it, but Waters had his knife in his hand, and he dragged the blade ferociously across the enemy soldier's back, slashing an opening in the man's EVA suit at least two feet long, and slicing into his chitinous torso, and oh, heavens, did the blood pour forth from that.

Then Waters grabbed the suit's fabric at one side of the opening and pulled it wide open. This all happened so fast, it was hard for me to follow it. It was a decidedly unpleasant way for one to lose his life.

I MOVED to the opening in the deck, firing my shotgun into it repeatedly. I looked intently into the hole, and I could see into the well-lit interior of the boarding craft. I saw no enemy, but then, quick as a chimney swift, an enemy soldier passed beneath me inside the boarding ship. I shot at him twice, and then I noticed his reason for that stunt.

He had tossed a grenade up through the opening.

It hit my shin and then slid down to the deck, near my feet. This was one of the particularly cruel weapons that the Kerleegans used when boarding. It was an incendiary anti-personnel grenade, designed to throw out a spray of a burning compound which simply could not be extinguished. It supplied its own oxygen, and woe betide you if a drop of it landed on your suit.

I had only one thought: Get that grenade back where it came from. I put my boot against its side, and I scooped it back through the opening, into the enemy ship. I yelled, "Grenade!" I leaped as far away from it as possible.

The explosion wasn't loud, because we only got what little sound was transmitted through the solid parts of the ship, and up into our suits, through our boots and bodies. But through the corner of my eye, I saw the spray of molten compound that shot back up into the *Valley Forge* from the grenade's detonation inside the boarding craft.

40

THE CLEVER SAILORS

As soon as the explosion was over, I jumped to my feet, because I knew we needed to give that hole in our hull more attention. And right next to me was one of our sailors, and cradled in his arms was one of our Coffin Nail guided-missiles, with which we sometimes armed our Banshees. They were four feet long and weighed about a hundred pounds, and they existed in incendiary versions and explosive versions. The nose of this one was painted a brilliant orange, so this was an incendiary.

The sailor looked me in the eye, and then he looked at the side of the missile, toward the safety device. It was an arm-fire mechanism that armed the missile without the requirement of high missile-velocity. I grabbed the handle, twisted it, and yanked it off.

Then I extended my arms to help him with the missile, and without delay we carried it ten feet to the opening, tipped it nearly vertical, and released it. Then we both turned and dove face-down away from the hole. Everyone else was already flat.

Well, the contact fuse worked to perfection, and from where we were, the noise of the explosion was beautifully loud, having been transmitted through the frameworks of the ships. The deck shook violently, and the compartment was lit brightly.

I grabbed my shotgun and sprang back to the opening, and the sight I saw was a welcome one. The Kerleegan ship's hold on the *Valley Forge* had been released, and their ship was drifting away from us in space. I could easily see the enemy craft's open hatch through which their soldiers had been boarding.

The opening and much of the interior of the enemy craft were illuminated by the inferno caused by the incendiary. I don't know whether any of the enemy survived that blast, but I imagine that the survivors, if any, were an unhappy group.

Good. They had it coming.

A lot of our people were cheering. The regular crewmen were especially vocal, and they were all high-fiving each other and slapping one another on the back for their creative use of the missile. I certainly admired them for that. But I couldn't join in the celebration, because I was too busy making sure all of us were alive. I looked from person to person. All of us were indeed still living, and I saw no signs of anyone being wounded.

We had some mop-up work to do. The crewmen gathered the enemy weapons and put them aside for close examination later, and then they helped the Marines drop the four enemy bodies one by one back through the hole, into the blackness of space.

I shook hands with the four sailors, as did the others. In fact, the sailors formed a line, and in another separate line were the Marines and midshipmen. The two lines shook hands. It was something like the end of an NHL playoff-game. Only difference was we were all on the same team. And then I knew I had to get back to Rabinowitz and the other commanders, to see whether they had any particular ideas that we needed to implement.

41

AMASSING IN THE BAYS

Back in the midshipmen's ready-room, only Rabinowitz was present. She was monitoring several screens, one of which showed the activity in section N. But she had been watching another screen momentarily and missed the key happenings. She said she heard the detonation and wondered what it was.

We told her about the creativity of her crewmen, and she smiled.

Rabinowitz told us that Silver and Newton were helping set up barricades with good lines of fire toward the four airlocks aft of the two fighter bays. Then she pointed to four monitors showing feeds from the two bays. It was clear that the enemy was amassing there.

Rabinowitz said to Waters, "I suggest you divide your men up at the barricades that are being constructed aft of the bays. Give the sailors there whatever help they seem to need."

Waters said, "Aye aye, Ma'am." Then he turned to his people and said, "You heard the commander. Let's move out, on the double."

Without a further word, the eight Marines rushed out. When they were gone, only Rabinowitz, Lennox, Nash, and I were still in the ready-room.

I wondered what Rabinowitz had up her sleeve for us three midshipmen. So far, she had shown us no preference whatsoever. She would just as soon have us students die as any other members of her crew.

I guess you have to be that way if you are going to command a starship. If I ever ended up in command of a starship, I don't think I would be able to be that cold. That was another example of me knowing that my approach to war was different than that of most.

I said, "Talos, what does the enemy plan seem to be?"

Talos said, "So far they've been moving through sections of the *Valley Forge* that are compressed. They've left the airlocks open at the point of entry to the fighter bays, so they are moving freely and quickly."

That surprised me, since I figured they would use the airlock function when entering the bay. For some reason, I assumed they probably would need it. They figured out that they *didn't* need it. They simply left everything compressed between the fighter bays and the airlocks nearest the boarding ships. So they were simply moving through the ship unbothered.

Rabinowitz said, "Talos, can you close all airlock hatches remotely?"

Talos said, "I can close or open all of them, or specified ones."

I breathed a sigh of relief. We still would be able to trap them in the fighter bays.

Talos said, "Additional information: We have a Kerleegan soldier entering a Banshee in the starboard fighter-bay."

Rabinowitz said nothing. She knew well that none of the ships would operate without someone inputting the day's password.

Talos said, "Also, be advised that among the final Kerleegan troops are several soldiers who are bringing aboard a heavy weapon of some kind. Analysis shows that it is likely a version of a weapon which the United States designates as the LU-18 Heavy Plasma Cannon."

At this point, I was ready for just about anything, so I wasn't surprised by this. Our colloquial name for the LU-18 was "The Annihilator." It was strictly an anti-personnel weapon. It fired donut-shaped configurations of plasma that grew larger with distance. At thirty feet the toruses would be about six feet across.

These plasma donuts heat the surrounding air to high temperature. A stream of such donuts will fry the EVA suit right off its wearer. The weapon often can be used to destroy an enemy soldier without seriously damaging the structure that surrounds him.

Rabinowitz said, "That's not good, but we'll be decompressing the bays before they have a chance to use it. Talos, give me a situation report on the enemy."

Talos said, "Two enemy boarding ships have been destroyed with all hands. Three other boarding craft are now attached to the *Valley Forge*. Each carried two pilots and one hundred boarders, for a total of three hundred boarders. All boarders are now aboard the *Valley Forge*, and most are now in the fighter bays."

Rabinowitz said, "Okay, got it."

"Also," Talos said, "in the port fighter bay, about ten enemy soldiers are leaving the bay and entering one of the bay's aft airlocks. They will need to decompress the lock before moving on, because the next corridor is decompressed. Also, that corridor contains one of our barricades, and many crewmen, as well as several Marines. Two hundred eighty enemy soldiers are now in the bays."

Rabinowitz looked at me, Lennox, and Nash.

The three of us stepped near her.

42

I CAN BLOW THE BAY DOORS

Rabinowitz said, "I believe that now is the time to slam the airlock hatches closed and open the bay doors. Any insights?"

I said, "Agreed."

Rabinowitz nodded and said, "Talos, how much time does it take to open the outer bay-doors? How quickly can you do it?"

"I can *blow* the outer doors," Talos said. "Call it one second."

"Let's take the two bays one at a time," Rabinowitz said. "First, close and seal the airlock hatches for the starboard bay. Do that now."

Talos said, "Done. Starboard-bay hatches closed and sealed."

"Now," Rabinowitz said, "blow that bay's outer bay-door."

I could hear the muffled sounds of the explosives that blew the bay-door.

"Is that bay door clear now?" Rabinowitz asked. "Can we decompress that bay?"

Talos said, "Indeed."

Rabinowitz said, "All right, now it's time to carry out the death sentence on the Kerleegans in the starboard bay." She paused, then said, "Talos, cut the forcefield."

Talos said, "Done."

I thought I felt the ship rock. I didn't hear a thing. But the view on the monitors told the story.

When Talos cut the forcefield that had kept that bay compressed, this caused a violent decompression of the bay. Theory says that, when measured at the bay opening, the air initially exits at almost precisely Mach 1. During a time of about two seconds, over a hundred soldiers were sucked out of the bay, into space—or rather were shoved out by the exiting air.

Where there had been a hundred and forty or more enemy soldiers in the bay, I now saw six or seven. And they weren't standing, and they weren't moving.

I continued to look closely at the monitor, trying to determine whether there were any survivors. The magnets had held the Banshees in place, for the most part, though some had scooted a little distance, and one was even tipped at an angle. Some of the boarders had collided forcefully with the Banshees and were either knocked over or killed. But for the most part, the bay looked strangely peaceful.

"All right," Rabinowitz said, "next the port bay. Talos, close and seal those airlock hatches, now."

Talos said, "Aye aye, Ma'am." After a pause, Talos said, "The forward hatch of that bay will not close. Something is blocking it open."

Rabinowitz said, "Okay, that just means we'll decompress more of the ship than we wanted to. None of our people are in any of the areas that'll be decompressed. For now, go ahead and blow the outer bay-door."

Talos said, "I can't do that, Ma'am. It's a safety feature that I can't override. As long as that airlock's forward hatch is unsealed, the outer bay-door can't be blown."

Rabinowitz said, "Can it be done manually?"

"No."

I looked at Lennox and Nash and pointed my thumb upward.

We rose and grabbed our M90s. We slung those over the shoulder, and each of us grabbed a shotgun.

Talos continued. "The cameras covering that area have been disabled by the enemy. Scans give a poor image."

I said to Rabinowitz, "We'll take care of it."

Lennox, Nash, and I grabbed our helmets, and we were out of the ready-room before Rabinowitz even replied.

Once outside the ready-room, we put on our helmets. I was uncomfortable. Without the helmet, the suit was nothing you would want to wear for more than a few minutes. With the helmet on, you'd think my misery was complete.

But on top of that I was toting the shotgun, and I had the M90 slung on my right shoulder, and my cross-draw shoulder holster on my left side. With spare magazines for the M90, that's easily thirty pounds of weapons. Under normal circumstances, all this would border on unbearable. But in the middle of battle, I could almost ignore it.

I said, "Let's swing by the armory." I expected that

there would be a dozen or so Kerleegans in the corridor by the airlock hatch. It was a short detour to the armory, and we needed more than our M90s, and more than our shotguns.

The three of us entered the armory. I said, "What do you guys think?"

Lennox said, "Grenades. Incendiary grenades."

I said, "Sounds good. Nash and I can grab a crate of them."

43

INCENDIARY GRENADES

I slid a crate of the grenades out from under a table. I pulled it open and looked inside, to make certain it was what we wanted. I could see the top layer, four rows with five grenades in each row. The box held two layers, so there were forty grenades in all. The grenades weighed a little over a pound each, so with the crate this was about forty-five pounds.

Nash and I each grabbed a handle of the crate. The three of us moved out of the armory, toward the corridor leading to the fighter-bay. Lennox took point.

The incendiary grenades are brutal, savage weapons. Ours were especially fearsome, as they were white-phosphorus grenades with a napalm kicker. Their maximum effective radius was about thirty feet, but if you were within ten feet, it was time to say goodbye.

The napalm was an advanced formula, that, strictly speaking, was not napalm, though that's what we called it. Our stuff burned hotter and longer, and it sprayed more effectively.

The Kerleegans routinely used incendiaries when

boarding a ship, as well as in the course of ground combat. I personally didn't like the idea of using them in open-field combat, and our own regulations prohibited their general use.

But we had two exceptions. First, if the enemy used them, we would use them. Secondly, if the enemy boarded one of our ships, no holds were barred, and we were expected to use anything and everything to save the ship, regardless of how vicious it might be.

I said, "Talos, can you update us on how many enemy troops are located in the corridor near the airlock?"

Talos said, "Yes, Ma'am. There are eleven enemy soldiers near the airlock that I was unable to close and seal. The rest of that corridor is empty."

I asked, "How close are they to the airlock?"

"All are within thirty feet," Talos said. "I still cannot see the actual airlock hatch, but it is not the LU-18 that is holding it open. It is probably a smaller weapon or something else not easily crushed."

I said, "Then where is the LU-18?"

Talos said, "The enemy has mounted it on a tripod and aimed it at the next hatch. Their intent is evidently to defeat what you are trying to accomplish."

Lennox said, "Seems like we need a diversion. The bad guys will turn their attention to that, and we can swing open the corridor hatch and let 'em have it."

If we could come up with a suitable diversion, that would probably work. The corridor that led to the enemy soldiers was an enclosed straight passage. The hatchway nearest the enemy was the entryway to the fighter bay, or rather to the airlock that joined to the fighter bay.

The next hatchway—in the other direction down the corridor, toward us—was about sixty feet forward of them.

That was the hatchway that the enemy was watching.

It was also the hatchway that Lennox, Nash, and I needed to enter. Then we had to deal with the eleven Kerleegans and their LU-18. Then we needed to unblock the airlock hatch, and get the hatch closed and sealed.

Nash said, "I can use the catwalk that runs parallel to the corridor. When I'm roughly even with the LU-18, I can rap on the outside of the corridor. Maybe they'll at least look away from the gun for a second."

I said, "Any better ideas?" After a pause, I said, "Okay, then, that's the plan."

Soon we were in a maintenance area near the target corridor.

Nash stepped out onto the catwalk.

I said, "Don't fall, Nash."

He said, "Thanks for the reminder, Amundsen."

I patted him on the shoulder and said, "I'll let you know when we're in position."

"Got it," Nash said, and he moved out onto the narrow catwalk.

Lennox and I lugged the grenade crate to the forward hatch, the one we needed to go through. Our plan was to wait till we heard Nash's rapping. Talos, we hoped, would inform us that the enemy was distracted.

Our grenades were fully optimized for anti-personnel uses. They were truly murderous weapons, but since the life of the *Valley Forge* was at stake, my heart was flint.

Lennox readied one of the grenades by pulling the pin, but of course she kept the lever depressed.

I did the same to another grenade. I held it in my right hand.

Lennox transferred her grenade to my left hand, and even that little maneuver was scary, because any slip and we were in for a galaxy of hurt.

Then Lennox was standing at the hatch, with her gloved hands grasping the wheel firmly.

I said, "Nash, we're all set. Lennox and I are in position. Go, any time."

Nash said, "Three, two, one . . . ."

Immediately we heard the racket that Nash was dealing out.

Talos said, "Amundsen, go."

Almost before that was halfway spoken, Lennox had turned the hatch's wheel the necessary quarter turn, and she was yanking the hatch open.

In one motion, I stepped partially into the half-open hatchway and tossed the first grenade.

The quick glance I took seemed to show that all the Kerleegans were looking in the direction of Nash's disturbance, meaning that the LU-18 wasn't properly manned. I took a chance with another grenade. While I was throwing it, the first one ignited, and that became the focus of every Kerleegan I saw.

Then the second detonated.

I reached to the crate and grabbed another grenade.

Lennox could tell what was going on. She now had the hatch almost wide-open. Using it for partial cover, she began firing her shotgun into the crowd.

By this time, I had long since stopped hearing Nash's racket, but that didn't matter any more.

I threw a third grenade. This time I tried to launch it *over* the nearest part of the crowd. It would have made it to the airlock hatch, but it collided with someone, fell to the deck, and immediately exploded.

It took Lennox only a few seconds to empty the twenty-four round magazine of her shotgun.

Then she grabbed her M90.

As she was doing that, I threw another grenade.

Next thing I knew, Nash was beside me, grabbing a grenade from the crate. I stepped aside, and he threw it down the hall, hard.

The area down the hall was now filled with smoke, and it was difficult to see anything. I figured that waiting around was not a good idea, so I grabbed my M90 and moved quickly into the smoke. Nash and Lennox followed me.

I said, "I'm gonna try to get to the hatch and seal it."

44

TAKING CARE OF THE WOUNDED

We began encountering bodies. I figured that few, if any, of the Kerleegans had avoided significant contact with the white phosphorus and napalm. I thought maybe half of them would be dead, but I was sure that every one of them still living was in agony from the effects of the burning phosphorus.

When we got to the first body, I said, "Lennox and Nash, cover me." I wanted to see what damage the phosphorus had done, so that I could assess what the effects on the other ten Kerleegans might be.

Lennox moved into the smoke, which was starting to dissipate. I assumed that Talos had opened some ventilation ducts.

I quickly dragged the body to a less smokey area. As I did so, I could see the writhing bodies of three or four Kerleegans, who were trying, unsuccessfully, to extinguish the burning phosphorus and napalm.

I heard Lennox discharging her M90 in short bursts. I figured she was delivering death blows to Kerleegans who were still moving—at point-blank range, or more likely, with contact shots.

As for the body I was looking at, significant portions of his suit were burned away. The Kerleegans have what looks like an exoskeleton that covers their torsos, and the incendiary material had burned away a large section of that. This soldier's insides were exposed. He was plainly dead.

I moved forward past Lennox, and past the twisted mass of Kerleegan bodies, now intent on getting to the hatch as quickly as possible. I was ready with my M90, but found no cause for shooting it.

I soon reached the hatch. It was blocked open by a helmet. I looked into the airlock. Nothing was inside. The far hatch was open about an inch, and those within the fighter bay were trying to open it further, but to no avail.

I reached down and grabbed the helmet, thinking to remove it, but the hatch was closed tightly against it. I described the situation to Talos.

Talos said, "I've opened the hatch a little. Try now."

I did. The helmet came out, and I threw it down.

I slammed the hatch closed and twisted the wheel, sealing the hatch.

I said, "Hatch sealed."

Almost immediately, I heard the explosions from the blowing of the outer bay-door.

I looked through the windows of the airlock hatches as Talos cut the forcefield. It wasn't a perfectly clear view, but I saw scores of Kerleegan soldiers being swept rapidly across my field of view, out into space.

~

That concluded this phase of the battle. I thought and hoped that the battle might actually be over now, and that the Kerleegans would depart.

I was struck by the fact that this was somewhat anti-climactic. I had hoped that the decompressing of the two bays would have taken place without any difficulties, remotely.

But God intervened, I think to show me that if wars were conducted that way, we wouldn't see how ugly they really were.

I had thought I already knew that. Maybe this was a refresher course. So, Lennox and Nash and I had to get our hands dirty. As the French say, "*C'est la vie. C'est la guerre.*" Such is life. Such is war.

By now, all the phosphorus had burned out. Much of the smoke had dissipated. The ventilation system had cleared it out pretty thoroughly.

Nash and Lennox were studying the eleven bodies, watching for movement. The bodies were mainly in a tangled mess, lying every which way.

I said, "This is pretty disgusting, but we better pull them apart and take care of any who aren't dead."

Nash said, in a burst of naiveté, "Take care of?"

Lennox said, "She means, you know, finish them off."

"Oh, right," Nash said.

I said, "Lennox, you keep watch over Nash and me, okay?"

She nodded.

I was exhausted, and it was difficult work, but Nash and I finally separated all of the bodies.

None of them were moving, and I was sure they were all dead. Still, I took my sidearm and pressed it against one of the bodies and discharged it twice. I did this to three of the bodies in all, so Lennox wouldn't think she was the only one who had killed wounded enemy soldiers.

Then it was time to move back to the ready-room. We abandoned the remaining grenades and our shotguns. We took with us our M90s and our sidearms.

45

YOU FORFEIT YOUR LIFE

When we arrived back in the ready-room, Rabinowitz said, "Good job, the three of you. I'm keeping the crew at the barricades until we know that the threat is gone. We're either waiting for more boarding craft, or for an indication from the enemy that this is over."

I said, "Well, I hope it's over. I'm worn out."

Talos said, "The six carriers and four of the cruisers are departing the area. All of the fighters have returned to the carriers. Two of the three boarding craft have separated from the *Valley Forge* and are moving out. One boarding craft remains, probably in order to remove survivors, if there are any who reach there."

Rabinowitz said, "Talos, seal the fighter bays back up. Begin recompression of all decompressed areas. Bleed pressure from sections that are still compressed, and also pump air into the system."

Talos said, "Will do, Ma'am."

I wanted to know about the Kerleegans who had entered the airlock that led from the port fighter-bay toward one of our barricades. They had made it closer to the stern than any of the others who entered the fighter bays. They were isolated in that airlock, without any workable alternatives.

I asked Rabinowitz, "What about the Kerleegans who entered that airlock? Looked like they wanted to head for the stern."

Rabinowitz said, "They surrendered. There are ten of them in custody."

Lennox said, "What happens to them?"

Rabinowitz said, "The law and the regs are clear. If you're captured while boarding one of our ships, you're executed. You forfeit your life."

For some reason, this made my stomach turn. I said, "But they're leaving. We've already killed, oh, I can't even add it up."

Talos said, "A reasonably close estimate is seventeen hundred."

I said, "There. And we can't let ten of their guys, who surrendered, mind you, continue to live?"

Rabinowitz said, "Regs are regs. This is not a time to be charitable. They have their way of fighting. Sometimes they don't fight to the last man. Those who remain may surrender." She paused, then added, "And we have *our* way of fighting. We execute them. Pretty simple."

I didn't reply. I knew the law and the regs as well as Rabinowitz.

So we had taken ten Kerleegan prisoners. I didn't know for certain whether any would actually be executed. The Navy would want to question them. And we might want to have them available to trade for some of our people, if the occasion arose. I wasn't too worried about anything like summary executions without any inquiry.

I said, "Any enemy left alive in either bay?" I continued to study the monitors that showed the starboard bay. It looked as though three or four enemy soldiers were unscathed. Probably they had been near the interior bulkhead, where the rush of air had been least powerful.

Rabinowitz said, "Waters is checking the bay you just came from. You want to look at the other bay?"

I didn't really want to, but I did want to be in control of whatever happened to any still-living Kerleegans who might be in that bay. I said, "Yes, Ma'am." I slung my M90 over my shoulder. About a dozen shotguns were nearby. I grabbed one of them.

Rabinowitz said, "Take Lennox and Nash."

I said, "Aye aye, Ma'am," and the three of us headed out to the starboard fighter-bay.

Honestly, I felt bitter about Rabinowitz's cold statements regarding executions. At least she could have expressed a hope that the executions wouldn't be carried out. Or she could have said she didn't like it any better than I did. *Anything* would have been better than "regs are regs."

I was also annoyed that Rabinowitz was simply running a pushbutton war from her place of safety in the ready-room. It was all basically, "Waters, go kill those people," or "Amundsen, make the enemy regret what they're doing."

Yes, I'm paraphrasing, but my point is that Rabinowitz wasn't the one tossing incendiary grenades into an enemy-held corridor, and she wasn't the one dropping a Coffin Nail missile into an enemy boarding ship, and she wasn't the one taking out a Banshee to launch missiles at incoming boarding craft, killing hundreds.

Rabinowitz did make at least one clear misstatement. She said that "we have *our* way of fighting."

Not true.

She has *her* way of fighting.

And I have *mine*.

46

CLEARING THE FIGHTER BAYS

My group soon reached the barricade located aft of the starboard bay, and it was wonderfully dense and protective, made up of everything from old chairs and desks, to heavy sheets of armor, which were in plentiful supply on the *Valley Forge*. It was all cleverly arranged in two levels, one behind the other, so that there was a fall-back position. We saw plenty of crewmen nearby, probably around thirty, plus four of the Marines.

With difficulty, Lennox, Nash, and I made our way through the barricaded area. About thirty yards in front of us was the airlock hatch. Between the hatch and us was a mass of concertina wire, and that is vicious stuff.

I didn't even know we had any of that on board. I assumed that it belonged to the Marines. It was an interesting arrangement of two coils stretched across the corridor, on the deck, and a third coil on top of those.

When we got halfway to the wire, a Marine caught up with us.

It was Alec. He patted my helmet and said, "Didn't really get a chance to talk with you after that section-N business. Thank God you made it, Astrid. You take awful chances. You should have been dead at least twice there. I was proud to be in there with you."

I said, "We were pretty lucky."

He tapped my weapon and said, "Told you, Astrid. Shotguns."

I said, "And we've fired quite a few rounds. What about this razor wire?"

Alec said, "That wire's all on a collapsible rack. I'll show you."

And sure enough, when we reached the razor wire, we could easily see the framework. Alec pulled a six-inch release-lever, and then Nash and Lennox and I helped collapse the thing, so that it was about three feet wide. Alec locked it into position, and we were able to get past it easily.

Alec said, "I better go with you."

I said, "No, thanks. You know, we midshipmen like to think we're making our own way in this world."

Alec laughed. He said, "This world? What on Earth does *that* refer to? Well, don't get killed at *this* stage of the game!"

I smiled and waved.

The airlock hatch was closed. The red light meant that the lock was decompressed. Since the corridor, the airlock, and the bay were all decompressed, Nash, Lennox, and I could have moved straight through the airlock and into the bay.

But we closed the hatch behind us, so that the lock would be back in its normal state. We then moved to the hatch that led into the bay. We looked through the hatch's window.

Four or five enemy soldiers were trying unsuccessfully to open up the airlock at the far end of the bay. Apparently they wanted to retreat to the one remaining Kerleegan boarding ship. None of them were holding weapons.

I said, "Talos, can you let those guys into the lock, so they can get out?"

Talos said, "Certainly. But they all have dropped their weapons, and it would be a simple matter for you three to eliminate them."

"What about taking them prisoner?" I asked.

Talos said, "We already have ten prisoners, some of whom appear to be leaders. If we need further prisoners, we can acquire more in the future."

I wasn't at all surprised to hear Talos say that. I said, "Who programmed you, anyway? We're not killing anyone else. The fight is over. Let me ask you this. If Lennox and Nash and I were in the situation these guys are in—say we had boarded an enemy ship, and we lost the fight, and now we wanted to depart for home—should the enemy execute us? Remember, it's Lennox, Nash, and I. We didn't kill anybody. We simply want to leave in peace, and hopefully live to see our families again. Would that be the right strategy for the enemy? Just kill us outright?"

"Yes, Ma'am."

I shook my head and said, "You *are* cold-blooded. Maybe you need to brush up on the Golden Rule."

"I know the Golden Rule, Ma'am," Talos said. "I don't follow it."

"Talos, forget it. Just let them into the lock."

"Yes, Ma'am."

We could see them enter the lock and close the hatch behind them.

I said, "We can enter the bay now. Everyone, high alert."

We entered. I had my shotgun. Nash also had a shotgun, and Lennox carried her M90. A quick look around showed no one anywhere on the deck of the bay, or at least no one living, as far as I could tell. We still needed to check the Banshees.

Talos said, "Enemy soldier in *Mabel's Nightmare*."

My ears perked up when I heard that, since *Mabel's Dream* was the ship I had piloted a little earlier. This one must have been a sister ship. The engine compartment was open, and I realized that this was one of the inoperable Banshees. The three of us approached the ship carefully.

No enemy soldier was immediately evident. I climbed up onto a wing, wondering what I might see. Cowering within the cockpit was the enemy soldier. I gestured with my shotgun for him to exit. The canopy popped open, and the soldier began to stand.

47

HE'S STILL ALIVE

I could see the guy's weapon there next to the pilot's seat, and I wondered whether he might go for it. That seemed unlikely. I had my shotgun pointed at him.

But he couldn't resist the temptation. He stooped over to grab it, and before he could even touch it, I had swung the stock of my shotgun around and delivered a stunning blow to his helmet. He stood back up, and I'm sure he thought I was going to unload my shotgun into him.

But I didn't.

The forward airlock popped open, and one of their people, weaponless, was running toward us.

The hatch behind him was open, and the airlock was devoid of Kerleegans, so unless they were just beyond the airlock, waiting to ambush us, they probably were returning to the boarding ship.

This new arrival from the airlock seemed to want to dissuade me from killing his friend, which I had no intention of doing.

The would-be pilot climbed down, and his friend

embraced him. I thought that was weird, but these guys weren't so different from us, I guess.

I said, "Talos, what's going on with the Kerleegans you released into the airlock? Looks like they left the lock."

"Yes, they are no longer in the area, and they are in fact near the remaining boarding craft."

I said, "Are any of these bodies here in the bay still alive?"

Talos said, "Ten paces to your left, one is alive."

I said, "Is the bay pressurized yet?"

Talos said, "Not quite at normal levels yet, but it's safe to remove helmets."

I lost no time removing mine. It was almost unbearably confining. Then I stood guard while Nash and Lennox removed theirs.

The Kerleegans kept theirs on.

I tapped one of the Kerleegans on the shoulder and pointed toward the body. Even though I was sure they couldn't understand me, or even hear me, I said loudly, "He's still alive."

The two Kerleegans and I walked over to the guy. I tried to help them get him up.

I should probably say that throughout this whole procedure, Nash and Lennox both had their weapons trained on these two enemy soldiers. But I wasn't worried. I knew that they only wanted to leave.

So we got the wounded soldier up. Then, to my surprise, one of the Kerleegans swung open his faceplate and said, "Thank you."

This was the first close-up view I had of a Kerleegan's face, other than in images. Overall the features were human-like, but somewhat smooth and expressionless.

His eyes were squinted, and his nose was not prominent. His lips were thin.

I was surprised to hear him speak, but this was good, because I could find out more. I said, "Is there a chance your ships will leave without you?"

He said, "No, one of the ships is staying behind."

I said, "What about your people in the other bay?"

The Kerleegan said, "I am told they have all departed the bay safely and are aboard our remaining ship."

That I found interesting. Waters and his people hadn't needed to kill anyone else, and not only that, Waters had allowed those present to return to their boarding craft.

I said, "As long as your people aren't leaving without you, we have time to get a stretcher."

The fighter bay had a ton of first-aid supplies and medical equipment, including a half-dozen stretchers.

I pulled a stretcher out of one of the lockers. I brought it over by the three Kerleegans, and I said, "This is basic. We have other stuff, but it would take a lot of time to set up, and I assume you want to get out of here."

The speaker said, "Thank you, but yes, we need to leave."

The Kerleegans placed their wounded friend onto the stretcher.

I said to Lennox, "Let's help them get to their ship. Nash, you can escort us. Be ready for anything."

48

LIMITED TRUST

I trusted these three Kerleegans—to some extent. I leaned my shotgun against one of the Banshees. So did Lennox. But we drew our sidearms.

Lennox took the front right-handle of the stretcher. I took the rear right. The Kerleegans took the left handles.

Talos opened the airlock hatch for us. We were able to do a pass-through, since most of the area we were moving through was compressed.

I figured I would try to find out more about these Kerleegans. I asked, "How many of your people speak English?"

The speaker said, "About one in five. When we are at war with a nation, it is required that a good number of us learn their language—probably because of situations like this one."

I said, "And why are you at war with the United States? In *your* view."

He laughed in a human-like manner, and he said, "You are asking the wrong person. If it were up to me, we would not be at war. But you Americans are a warlike people."

"No, not so much," I said. "We fight to defend ourselves, and our allies."

The Kerleegan was skeptical. "All right."

I said, "Would a warlike nation let you go?"

"That I cannot answer, but my fleet had no intention of attacking you, until you changed course to intercept us. We had been on our way home."

I thought about Captain Jefferson's fiddling with the controls of the *Valley Forge*. He definitely had intended to engage these guys. I said, "The situation wasn't as simple as you believe."

"It's always *something*, isn't it? But you are letting us leave in peace, so *you*, at least, are not warlike."

I wanted to like this guy, but he was making it mighty hard. He needed to refute everything I said.

On the other hand, I was directly responsible for the deaths of three hundred of his people, and I played a key role in the deaths of over two hundred more. I avoided pointing that out to him.

I said, "You speak of home. Where might that be?" I tried to ask this casually.

"That, I am not permitted to tell you," he said. "But I can tell you it is far away."

"In this galaxy?" I asked.

He didn't answer. I hate it when people do that type of thing.

We trudged along until we came to another airlock. I knew we were about to enter a decompressed section of the ship.

I said, "Is that your exit there, on the other side of this lock?"

He nodded. "Yes, it is."

We set the stretcher down so that Lennox, Nash, and I could put our helmets on. Before we did that, though, the five of us had one last conversation—the soldier on the stretcher seemed unconscious. So, it was just we three midshipmen and the two enemies from the fighter bay. We said farewells.

I said, "Is your friend going to be okay?"

One of them said, "Yes, I am sure. We have highly advanced medical procedures."

I said, "Good. Maybe someday your people will share some of those procedures with us. Ours are kind of primitive."

The enemy soldier laughed. "You are peaceful, and funny. Still, I hope that will happen someday, perhaps soon."

I clutched the hand of each of them and wished them calm seas. They wished the same to us.

Lennox, Nash, and I put our helmets on, and our enemies sealed their faceplates. We used the airlock for a safe passage into the final area. The opening in the *Valley Forge*'s deck and hull was right ahead.

Two more Kerleegan soldiers came up out of the boarding ship, waving a piece of white cloth, which I thought was a good idea. They helped bring the wounded Kerleegan aboard their ship.

Each of the enemy soldiers briefly held up a hand, and we returned the gesture. Then they climbed down a ladder into their ship. A hatch closed behind them, and we heard a clanking sound as their ship separated from the *Valley Forge*.

I was disappointed.

In those days—not that long ago—I was far more optimistic and positive about . . . everything. I had thought our Kerleegan "friends" would show more appreciation for the fact that we were releasing them. On some level, I had expected them to ask us to join hands and sing "Kum Ba Yah, My Lord," or maybe share with us some ancient rite of peace from their nation.

As it is, I suppose I should be glad that they didn't toss a couple of their incendiary grenades into the *Valley Forge* as a Parthian shot.

49

CAPTAIN JEFFERSON'S FATE

We made it back to the ready-room without further incident. Rabinowitz, Silver, and Newton were all there, as were Waters and all the other Marines.

Waters verified that all of the survivors of the decompression incident in the other bay had "escaped." Rabinowitz informed us that our so-called rescue ships would arrive in a period of hours. Plainly they had not been in any position to help us at all.

Commander Rabinowitz said, "Now we have to decide what to do about Captain Jefferson."

One of the Marines said, "Well, I gather there was some weirdness, but I myself don't have any first-hand information."

Lennox said, "Same with me."

Rabinowitz said, "That's all right. We're talking small units here, and we have to include everyone." She looked at Waters and said, "Talos told me about how you handled things on the bridge with Captain Jefferson. I'm proud to have you and others like you on this crew. Now, everyone, listen."

Commander Silver said, "Just a moment, Ma'am, maybe we could first get an update on the enemy. Are they really withdrawing?"

Rabinowitz said, "I'm sure they are. Talos?"

"Yes, Ma'am," Talos said. "The boarding ships are now well away. Most of the Kerleegan fleet have departed the area, as have all of the fighters. One cruiser has stayed behind at a distance of two thousand miles from the *Valley Forge*, presumably to pick up the boarding ships. If they planned to reengage, this behavior would make no sense."

Rabinowitz said, "All right, thank you." Then she said to us, "We could talk about the Captain Jefferson situation for hours. Here's the problem as I see it. It appears that Captain Jefferson snapped. We don't know why. His decision to engage the Kerleegans was contrary to the Navy's norms in these situations. I believe that his actions were brought about by some aberration in his thinking. But putting that aside, there was nothing unlawful about his orders."

Commander Newton said, "I suppose that's true."

"But Ma'am," Silver said, "what are you getting at?"

"That's what I'm trying to figure out," Rabinowitz said. "If we had followed Captain Jefferson's orders to the letter—if we had implemented course twenty-one, twenty-five—we would not have been worse off than we are now. For that matter, the Navy will look upon this battle as one that was highly successful for the United States."

"We lost thirteen men," Newton said.

"To the Department of Defense and to the Navy," Rabinowitz said, "that's nothing. They'll send American flags to the families, and that will be the end of it. And what other cost was there to us? We expended all our missiles, but not one was wasted. We destroyed hundreds of their missiles, hundreds of their fighters, and hundreds of their personnel."

Newton said, "Not sure where you're going with this."

"When I started talking," Rabinowitz said, "I didn't *know* where I was going. But the more I talk, the more it looks like Captain Jefferson was in the right, or at least as though all of his actions will be supported by the Navy."

Silver said, "That makes us, what? Mutineers?"

Rabinowitz said, "Talos, tell us what constitutes a mutiny."

Talos said, "A mutiny exists when two or more people refuse to obey orders, or do violence, or cause a disruption, with the intent to override lawful military authority."

Rabinowitz said, "Commander Newton and Commander Silver, both of you ended up in the brig, as did I, for our refusal to obey Captain Jefferson. That has the flavor of mutiny to me."

This discussion had take a turn completely different from what I had expected. I had thought that Commander Rabinowitz would style everything as Captain Jefferson's fault. She would gather us together, and tell us that we would cover for him, poor man, even if that meant authorizing Talos to modify his code and destroy his records of what really happened. And I pictured Waters, Nash, and me supporting her wholeheartedly in such a gracious move.

But now things were different. And, of course, being the hypocrite that I am, I immediately started looking down on Rabinowitz, Silver, and Newton—I, who had hoped against hope that they would overthrow the captain, by violence if necessary. I now saw them as little more than traditional mutineers: thugs and ruffians whom I wouldn't trust to walk my little sister across the street—if I had a little sister.

I shook my head in an effort to clear my mind of such evil thoughts. And, as a matter of fact, a great deal depended on the interpretation of events. I decided to say something.

"Commander Rabinowitz," I said, "may I offer an observation?"

Rabinowitz said, "You may."

I said, "I don't know much about the legal technicalities of what constitutes a mutiny and what doesn't. Now, I have zero knowledge as to what went on between Captain Jefferson on the one hand, and Commanders Silver and Newton on the other. But before anyone concludes that there was a mutiny, or even insubordination, it seems to me that the actual circumstances need to be considered. What I saw, primarily, was your desire to carry out the intent of the protocols that required you to make an independent determination as to whether or not you would affirm the captain's orders. No mutiny. That's all I have. Oh, also, there's the little matter of Captain Jefferson drawing his sidearm, taking the safety off, and racking the slide. That's got to mean *something*."

There was some mumbling among several of those present. I hadn't mentioned the pistol business to anyone else, and I had intended not to, and I'm sure that information was a surprise to most of those present.

"All right, thank you, Midshipman Amundsen," Rabinowitz said. "We'll write our reports and let the chips fall where they may. Any objection?"

No one said anything.

"All right, then, you may all resume your ordinary duties. Let's try to get the ship into decent condition. Lieutenant Waters, please see that all of the captured weapons are brought to the armory, including that LU-18. Talos, let everyone know that general quarters will remain in effect until further notice."

50

LOOKING BACK

And so, my adventure on the *Valley Forge* came to an end.

Talos continued to track the Kerleegan ships. They continued away from us, and they were running their engines during much of that, so they were easy to track. About five hours after their departure, they were well over a million miles away. At that time, Rabinowitz canceled general quarters.

As for our reinforcements—our rescue ships—I'm told they made radio contact with us about twenty hours after general quarters was first announced. That was about a half-day after the Kerleegans disappeared. The rescuers finally arrived at the *Valley Forge* about four hours after that.

I heard that Commander Rabinowitz had some choice words for the leader of the reinforcements. They had a lot of excuses. As my Kerleegan friend said, "It's always *something*, isn't it?"

Since the *Valley Forge* had expended all its missiles, all its drones, and all its countermeasures, it was less than pointless for us to go anywhere other than low Earth orbit, where repairs could be made to the ship, and she could be rearmed. That being the case, we piggy-backed on one of the cruisers that had arrived, and within a few days, Lennox, Nash, and I were back at the Academy.

~

What about sleep, soon after the battle?

Before the battle, even before general quarters was announced, I was thoroughly exhausted. I finally hit the rack about ten hours after the start of the battle. I slept for twelve hours.

Since Lennox's and my berth was occupied by the captain and a couple of medicos, we slept on couches in the ready-room.

I dreamed of summertime in California, and of beaches, and family, and Joseph, and there wasn't any war, and no one died.

~

In the end, no one was court-martialed. The Navy decided that the events on the bridge were ambiguous enough that no charges could be pressed. The Navy tends to back the captain in cases where there is any doubt, and they simply determined that Captain Jefferson had been ill. Whether the illness was physical or mental wasn't specified in any public report, as far as I know.

The pistol incident that took place on the bridge never made it into any official findings, as far as I have been able to determine. The same can be said regarding the discussion Jefferson had with Admiral Farragut.

Maybe no one on the crew mentioned those things in their reports. I know *I* didn't.

I'm glad to say that Captain Jefferson's future looks favorable. I hear that his mind is sharp again, and that he is as mean as ever, to *everyone*. So you could say he's back to normal. I have gone from tolerating him to respecting him, but more than anything else, feeling sad for him.

The medical people, so I'm told, made an all-out effort to determine the cause of Jefferson's mental breakdown. I have heard that he contracted some sort of alien virus, though that is only rumor. Whatever they find out, I doubt that it will become public information.

One of the most interesting aspects of the whole series of events was that Captain Jefferson was awarded the Congressional Medal of Honor for leading Nash, Lennox, and me in the attack on the Kerleegan boarding ships. I can't say he didn't deserve it.

Not only that, but Nash, Lennox, and me were awarded the Navy Cross for that same action. And thus I received the medal that Captain Jefferson was going to recommend me for. I suppose the three of us earned them. Others also deserved decorations, but didn't receive them. And I'm thinking about Adler and Boyle, among others.

Lennox, Nash, and I returned to Annapolis and managed to survive the remainder of our fourth year. As one might imagine, the three of us became much closer friends than we had been before our assignment to the *Valley Forge*.

In accord with my original plan, I applied for assignment to the Marine Corps on graduation from Annapolis. That was granted, and I was commissioned a second lieutenant.

After graduation, I chose the personal swearing-in. Joseph, my fiancé, administered the oath. A few weeks later, we were married in the chapel at the Academy, as planned.

Oh, a few final thoughts.

If you are ordered to kill, and you kill, and that's all there is to it, then you have given up your humanity, right?

I choose not to give up the things that make me a woman—or which make a man, a man. Whatever my orders, I will do my best to carry them out, but I will carry them out *my way*. I won't stop being human. At some point, this war stopped being just "a" war.

It became my own war, within a war.

My personal war.

Astrid's war.

Semper fi!

ADDENDUM

After writing the foregoing, I came into possession of information that sheds further light on Captain Jefferson's behavior. As I mentioned earlier, Jefferson said that the "key" element in determining our strategy was the idea that "the enemy has concluded a gravity-assist maneuver and their ships are now at zero acceleration." At the time, that made no sense whatsoever.

But yesterday I paid a visit to the Navy's Space War Records Center, to see what else I could find out about the Kerleegan attack on the *Adirondack*, during which Captain Jefferson's son was killed. I already believed that Jefferson's break was caused by the fact that the task force that attacked us had the same makeup as that which attacked the *Adirondack*.

In the files at the records center were transcripts of most of the communications that originated on the *Adirondack* before and during the attack. Most of that was classified Top Secret, and I didn't have access to it. But the final communication from the bridge before general quarters was announced was as follows: "Six carriers. Four cruisers. All have concluded a gravity assist and are at zero acceleration."

Thus the unfortunate similarity between the situation faced by the *Adirondack* and the *Valley Forge* went beyond the mere makeup of the enemy task force. That transmission I quoted was undoubtedly the reason Jefferson attached so much importance to the factors he considered "key."

—A.A.

December 2370

THE END

ACKNOWLEDGMENTS

Cover credits: Cover design by Elizabeth C. Sawyer, incorporating modified versions of images by Jessica Truscott (faestock) [foreground] and GrandeDuc [background], via Shutterstock.

Thank you to Elizabeth C. Sawyer, who kindly read three different versions of the first part of *Astrid's War*, and who gave me helpful comments. Also, thank you to Julie C. Gilbert, who read the entire manuscript and gave me the benefit of her comments. Julie's website:

www.juliecgilbert.com

ABOUT ALAN HOUSEHOLDER

Writing has long been one of Alan Householder's main passions. He recently published a young adult novel set in London in the late 1800s. He has written more than a dozen non-fiction works, principally on historical matters or book-related topics.

Alan is a graduate of the University of California, Los Angeles, and he is interested in the history of early UCLA football (roughly 1919-1939). He collects old books, and also illustration art from around a century ago.

Alan lives and writes in southern California.

Connect with Alan . . .

https://alanhouseholder.com
Write to Alan: alanhouseholderauthor@gmail.com

BONUS CONTENT

EXTRACT FROM
BOARDING PARTY:
THE BOARDING OF THE USS INVICTA
by Alan Householder

On the following pages may be found an extract from Alan Householder's forthcoming book *Boarding Party: The Boarding of the USS Invicta.* It is a section from around the middle of the book. This extract is recent, but it is subject to change.

Boarding Party picks up Astrid Amundsen's story after her graduation from Annapolis, and after some post-graduate work. She has opted to serve as a Marine, and she has been assigned to the USS *Invicta*.

The book is now available for pre-order on Amazon. The projected release date is January 14, 2020.

BOARDING PARTY, CHAPTER 25
SUPERSTITION

The arrival of the new intelligence about the Kerleegan fighters gave everyone a newfound enthusiasm, since we had the impression that the people back in DC actually gave a rap about what we were doing. This being the case, my people were taking the Banshees out more often than required, on their own initiative.

The day after our briefing regarding the Kerleegan craft, I pulled Downs into the pilots' ready-room for a discussion. We took our usual places at the table. Downs seemed energized and happy.

I said, "So, Downs, you seem particularly buoyant today."

"More than usual?" he asked. "I'm always an upbeat guy."

I said, "No, Downs, you're not. Not always. But I wanted to point something out to you."

"Do it."

"We've been out here for seven or eight weeks. All six

of us Marines are still alive. What do you have to say about that?"

"Uh, *ix-nay*, Astrid. You don't talk about a no-hitter when it's in progress. You'll jinx it."

I was a little irked by that. I said, "Look, Downs, why don't you make a list of your various superstitions, and those of the rest of the squad, and let me have the list. That way, I'll know in advance what I can say and what I can't say. To use a sports analogy like you did, can you please quit moving the goalposts?"

"Astrid, I don't think you understand just how sneaky and subtle and complex a superstition can be. And I use the term 'superstition,' because that's the term *you* used. But it doesn't really fit, since a *superstition* is something that is believed to be true, but which is actually false."

I said, "You're kidding."

"I *told* you *I* didn't believe it, but it looks like the others do."

"So you're the go-between, linking the supremely wise and rational Astrid with the weak-minded other members of the squad?"

Downs said, "That's a harsh way of putting it."

"I'm *not* putting it that way. I'm showing how absurd your point of view is. *You're* the main one who is promoting this whole superstition thing."

Downs shrugged.

I said, "Downs, it's been more than eight weeks since the most recent death. Period. The superstition, or curse—"

"Yes, curse," Downs said. "That's the term I would use."

"Okay, the curse called for someone to die every week or two. You lost seven people over a period of eight or nine weeks. And now we've gone eight or nine weeks with how many deaths? The total should be *all* the rest of A-Squad. We *all* should be dead. Let me see. Oh yeah, zero have died. None."

Downs said, "Your point?"

I shook my head in exasperation. "My point is there's no curse!"

"Well," Downs said, "I admit you have some evidence. But nothing conclusive."

I said, "Okay, Downs, go do whatever you would be doing if we'd never had this meeting. I give up."

"Okay, Astrid," Downs said. "Good little meeting."

Downs was being a jerk. I said, "It wasn't a good meeting, Downs. Get out of here."

Downs stood and moved toward the exit to the ready-room. When he reached the hatchway, he turned back toward me and said, "If we go another, oh, three weeks without losing anyone, then I might agree with you."

I said, "Why does the next three weeks make any difference?"

Downs said, "Well, you just applied what I call a *curse accelerator*. A curse doesn't want to be treated lightly. If it exists, one of us will die, and soon. If there is no curse, then we'll all be alive three weeks from now."

I said, "What if one of us dies, and it was just a death, not related to the curse?"

"We'll cross that bridge when we come to it. And I wouldn't keep using all those words relating to dying. Bad luck."

I said, "Nice mature analysis, Downs. You can go play with your building blocks now."

"Thanks, Mommy."

With that, Downs left, and I was glad to see him go.

He was in a good mood throughout our discussion, so much so that I was sure that he was just jerking my chain.

After Downs departed, though, I thought things over. Was there a curse in effect now? Had there been one before, one that brought about the deaths of seven squad members? Even without any deep analysis, I *knew that there was no such curse.* However, it did all seem weird. And people are superstitious, and sometimes their beliefs in superstitions can bring about their undoing.

BOARDING PARTY, CHAPTER 26
LAUNCH FAILURE

In recent days, we had come under increasing attack from isolated Kerleegan ships, generally one-man fighters. "Attack" is probably the wrong word. You could say that they invaded our space, and we considered it to be an act of aggression if one of their smaller craft came within two thousand miles of us. This "aggression radius" grew larger, depending on the number of enemy ships, their size, and their speed of approach.

But anyway, if there were only one small ship, this ordinarily didn't mean anything. Usually it was just a taunting by the enemy. Still, we had to respond in some way, and it was as though we were following a script. But two or three times we ended up destroying the enemy craft if they became too threatening.

We were never too worried during these encounters, but it always gave you a nervous feeling in the pit of your stomach, because you didn't know for certain whether the enemy had some super-bomb mounted to a little craft. That's why these jaunts were a bad idea for the enemy.

The more they did it, the less tolerant we were, and the more apt we were to engage and destroy them.

When we detected two (or more) craft, we always went out with the intention of destroying them. We couldn't afford to give them the benefit of the doubt. These were true "pushbutton" confrontations. We never saw the enemy, except as pinheads on our monitors. We launched missiles when we were around fifteen hundred miles out. Usually, the enemy would flee when they detected the incoming missiles. If they allowed our missiles to come within three hundred miles (which didn't happen much), it was usually game over, and they would simply disappear from our monitors. I know it sounds cold, but the enemy knew what they were up against.

The day after my meeting with Downs, we detected two enemy-craft several thousand miles out, so we scrambled three Banshees, and that day it was Pine, Lamar, and me. When we weren't in a tense situation, usually one of us would launch a missile, and then we would wait around and watch our monitors. Normally the enemy would flee.

When we got eight hundred miles away from the *Invicta,* I said, "Pine, go ahead and launch."

Pine said, "Aye aye, Ma'am. Launching one Piranha."

I looked at my monitors. Pine had initiated the launch, but I saw no missile. Then this message appeared on my monitor: "Ship 2, ventral A, failure to launch."

The "A" missiles were forward missiles, and the "B" missiles (when present) were mounted behind them. And today there was indeed a ventral B-missile on Pine's Banshee.

Pine said, "Ma'am, launch failure."

I said, "So I see."

We considered such a launch failure to be one of the worst things that can happen, because it means things aren't going according to plan on that missile, and you never know what's going to happen next. So, I added, "Go ahead and release the missile."

That was our normal next step—abandon the missile —if it could be made to separate, and often it couldn't.

Pine said, "No go."

My monitor now showed that the enemy ships were departing the area, so we didn't really need a launch. But we still had Pine's problem to deal with. This type of thing didn't happen often, but when it did, the protocol was to dock on the dorsal surface of the main ship—in this case, the *Invicta*—and to send a weapons man up to figure out what went wrong. In other words, keep the Banshee out of the fighter bay until the problem is resolved.

I said, "Okay, break all circuits for that missile. When we reach the *Invicta*, Lamar and I will enter the bay. Pine, you dock, and enter the *Invicta* through the docking port. See you guys once we land."

Then I contacted Drayton, who was the *Invicta*'s main missile-launch technician, and I alerted him to the problem.

BOARDING PARTY, CHAPTER 27
ANYBODY'S GUESS

When we arrived back at the *Invicta*, Drayton was in his EVA suit with magnetic boots, and he was standing near the docking port at which Pine was to dock. Next to him was a large tool-case.

Lamar entered the fighter bay.

I hovered near the docking port, just to make certain that everything went smoothly. Though we usually ran dark, having lights on wasn't dangerous at the moment, and the entire docking-port area was illuminated by floodlights.

Pine lit her cockpit lights, and I lit mine. She waved to Drayton, then docked, and finally disappeared downward as she moved to the Banshee's exit-port.

I also waved to Drayton, then brought my Banshee into the fighter bay, maneuvering with my RCS thrusters.

So far, so good.

Pine joined Lamar and me in the fighter bay.

When she arrived, Lamar and I were laughing about something. I forget what it was. Whatever it was, it was the wrong thing to be doing when Pine arrived, because she was in bad condition.

All the color was gone from her face. She looked almost like a corpse, and for her that represented a major change, since she was usually attractive and rosy-cheeked. She had a distant stare in her eyes, and she seemed barely able to walk.

Lamar and I each rushed to her side and took an arm. We walked her back to a chair and got her seated.

I said, "Gloria, what's wrong?"

Pine said, "I don't know. It hit me right after I entered the *Invicta*. If that missile can refuse to launch, well, it's disobeying, you know? I know it's just a machine, but still. And if it can do that, it can do anything. The warhead might detonate at any time."

She was right, of course, but an unwanted detonation was highly unlikely. I said, "Gloria, it doesn't work that way. There are a hundred safety features that keep that from happening." Right after saying that, I regretted it, because there aren't a hundred safety features, and Pine knew it. In reality, the number is around seven, and most of those are released when the Banshee is in flight.

Pine said, "I don't know," and then she said it again.

I said, "Look, Gloria, Drayton's checking it out. Let's at least hear what he has to say, okay?"

Pine said, "Astrid, it's the curse Downs talks about. I'm sure of it. It was trying to kill me. Next time it's not going to fail."

"There is no curse, Gloria," I said. "I'm sure of it."

"You are?" She spoke weakly, timidly. This was completely unlike her usual self.

"Yes," I said, "one hundred percent positive."

Some of the color was now returning to Pine's face. She seemed to be growing more stable. She looked up at Lamar and said, "Lamar, what do *you* think?"

In soft and confident tones, Lamar said, "Gloria, I have never been more certain of anything in my life, when I say I am absolutely certain that there is no curse, and that Lieutenant Amundsen is correct in everything she said." Then he paused, and added, "Except that there aren't a *hundred* safety features—but there are plenty."

At this, Pine smiled weakly and said, "Okay, good enough."

About an hour later, Drayton contacted me. He said, "Lieutenant, I think I found the problem." He explained that he had located part of a slug or some similar projectile from an earlier confrontation with the Kerleegans. It had penetrated the casing of the missile mount, and it had sliced into a connector, so that the circuit for the launch couldn't be completed.

I said, "Okay, but why would Pine's missile system have registered 'ready,' at takeoff?"

Drayton said, "Yeah, that's weird. I think there was minimal conductivity through the projectile fragment—enough to indicate that the system was in order, but not enough to cause the launch."

I said, "You really think that makes any sense at all?"

Drayton shook his head. "Not really. All I can say is, I took care of the repair of the problem I noted. Officially, everything is shipshape now. Just what I mean by that, though, is anybody's guess."

I said, "I get you. Thanks for what you did. Do you want to bring the ship into the fighter bay?" Drayton was a qualified pilot—not for combat, but for routine activities.

"Glad to."

~

I CONTACTED Pine and recounted my discussion with Drayton. We were all satisfied. We adopted an "all's well that ends well" attitude, which is so often the position we fall back on when we don't know what really happened.

I just hoped that the problem with the Banshee's missile-launch system wasn't deeper and more subtle. Drayton was the best in his specialty, but he wasn't all that certain that the real problem had been found, or was even findable. If I had unlimited resources, I probably would have destroyed both the Banshee and the missile, to play it safe. On the other hand, even new factory-fresh Banshees sometimes exhibited problems, so it's all a game you can't win.

Ultimately, I had Drayton check the missile-launch systems on all of the Banshees. I also had four electronics guys go over all the key electronics on all six Banshees. Lastly, I had a crew check and double-check everything mechanical. Well, "everything" might be going too far. I had them do what we call a "forty-hour check," which is supposed to take forty man-hours, per ship. It's an intermediate-level check, but it's reasonably comprehensive. Unless an emergency arose, we weren't going to take any fighters out until all of them were determined to be shipshape.

So, multiple teams were on it, and they worked in

shifts. They managed to complete three of the Banshees in thirty hours. Then they moved on to the other three. On the first three, they found several minor maintenance problems, but none of them had posed any safety problems.

BOARDING PARTY, CHAPTER 28
THE HOT-RUNNER

Pine's Banshee was one of the first three that Drayton's people finished with, as was mine.

A couple of hours after that, Pine and I were out in our Banshees, on what we called a routine patrol. It was mainly a dry run, to make certain that everything was in working order. I saw no cause for concern. I expected to return to the *Invicta* after about twenty minutes.

Everything went fine for the first fifteen minutes. But then, just as I was beginning to feel good, a rocket blast came from one of the missiles mounted under Pine's fighter.

Pine clicked into my line and said, "Astrid, I got a hot-runner forward of my ventral B-missile."

This was the very nightmare I had feared after Drayton and I decided that Pine's missile launch problem had been resolved. A "hot-runner" is a missile whose engine ignites unexpectedly while it's still mounted to the fighter.

Since the hot-runner was forward of the B-missile, that meant that the rocket blast of the malfunctioning missile was engulfing the warhead of the B-missile, as well as its fuel compartments. The A-missile had not accepted the launch command when it was made, a day earlier. Now, for some reason, the command was accepted, without Pine initiating it, and without the missile releasing from the Banshee.

This looked to be one of those rare instances of three or four unlikely things going wrong at once.

Realistically, Pine was as good as dead.

I tried to think. I had never confronted this situation before. Still, I had my training to fall back on.

I said, "Pine, you need to get free of the cockpit, now!"

"I can't. No EVA suit."

I knew that. Not sure why I made that suggestion. I then said, "Rotate one-eighty."

The Piranhas have an anti-circular-run mechanism that keeps them from circling back around after launch. In theory, the Piranha's engine will shut off if the missile reaches an angle of greater than ninety degrees variance from its angle at ignition. This normally didn't help when the missile was still mounted to the fighter, but it was worth trying.

Within seconds, Pine's ship was pointed in the opposite direction. Nothing happened. The rocket blast continued.

It was weird and frightening to see the full blast of the forward Piranha's engine enveloping the missile immediately in back of it—and knowing there was someone in the cockpit.

[End of Extract.]

Read more in Alan Householder's *Boarding Party: The Boarding of the USS Invicta.*

Boarding Party:
The Boarding of the USS Invicta
by Alan Householder

Book Two in the Astrid Amundsen Series

Release date: January 14, 2020
Special price until then!
Available for pre-order on Amazon,
or read for free on Kindle Unlimited.

Made in the USA
Las Vegas, NV
27 December 2023